PLAIN REVENGE

AN AMISH ROMANTIC SUSPENSE NOVEL

ALISON STONE

TREEHAVEN PRESS

All rights reserved.

No part of this book may be reproduced in any form or by any electronic or mechanical means, including information storage and retrieval systems, without written permission from the author, except for the use of brief quotations in a book review.

PLAIN REVENGE
Treehaven Press
Copyright © 2020 by Alison Stone

This book is a work of fiction. The names, characters, places, and incidents are products of the writer's imagination or have been used fictitiously and are not to be construed as real. Any resemblance to persons, living or dead, actual events, locale or organizations is entirely coincidental.

Be the first to learn about new books, giveaways, and deals by signing up for Alison's newsletter on her website: https://alisonstone.com/newsletter

Rev.B

❀ Created with Vellum

CHAPTER 1

Nerves fluttered in Eve Reist's belly and immediately she felt like a teenager again as she turned onto the familiar country road. She had hoped she would have grown a backbone in the hour drive from her apartment, but if anything her unease grew. Her stomach cramped, she could barely swallow from lack of saliva, and she had the first tingling of what she suspected might explode into an all-out anxiety attack if she didn't rein in her emotions. *Fast.* She was usually good at calming herself, something she had to do on a regular basis before she went live on air as a reporter for a local news station in Buffalo. However, there weren't any cameras here in Hunters Ridge. Just her family.

The one she had abandoned seven years ago.

The August sun hung low in the sky and already she felt twitchy about arriving at this late hour, making her feel like the rebel Amish teen that she had once been. Eve had honestly intended to get on the road immediately after her last Sunday morning shift, but a creepy fan had other plans. Why would anyone think it was appropriate to leave a disturbing message on the windshield? Her stomach had bottomed out at the sight of the angry black strokes ghosting through the thin paper, similar to the one left on her car when she'd stopped at a department store a week earlier:

I'm watching you.

Eve forced herself to loosen her grip on the steering wheel as the familiar ache in her shoulder blades returned. The first note had made her hyperaware of her surroundings, and the second one had her totally questioning her career path. It had taken everything in Eve to act chill and pluck the note out from under the wiper and carry it over to Mark, the station's security guard, as if it were a dirty tissue. Despite the juvenile handwriting and unsophisticated means to harass her, the creep knew how to sneak in and out of the secure parking lot without being seen. The memory sent a new shudder up her spine even after the guard's promise to double-check for blind spots on the video feed and make the appropriate adjustments.

Eve squinted against the lowering sun and slowed to go around a horse and buggy. She found herself angling her face away from the Amish driver, fearing someone would recognize her.

Recognize me. Eve chuckled. That was the entire problem with being an on-air reporter. Her mentor, Carol Oliver, had told her that this was part of the job, as if it were no big deal. The lost sleep and racing thoughts suggested otherwise. Carol was a broadcasting legend in Buffalo. She retired years ago but maintained deep connections in the business and cashed in on her fame with a full schedule of speaking engagements. Eve could imagine her now responding to Eve's concerns with a lifted hand, an enormous diamond sparkling on a thin finger while she doled out some droll advice along the lines of: "When people invite you into their homes on their insanely large TVs, you have to expect some of this nonsense."

Expect it, maybe. Like it, definitely not.

Eve was grateful, at least, that the station had a protocol in place to monitor these kinds of situations—and tie-in with the local police when necessary—in an effort to keep their employees safe.

Butterflies swarmed in Eve's belly as her childhood home came into view at the top of the crest. The large white farmhouse had a wide front porch complete with rocking chairs and a swing. It would have been picturesque if it hadn't been wrought with so much personal, emotional baggage.

Eve pressed the brake and eased onto the side of the country road. She let out a slow breath and wondered if she'd be able to take care of everything in two weeks—her allotted vacation. She knew she could stretch it into four, if necessary, but that seemed like a long time to stay in Hunters Ridge. She drummed her thumbs on the steering wheel and stared up at the house. The sun reflected in an upstairs window making her wonder, not for the first time, about how things could have been so very different for the young Amish girl who went to sleep each night in that same bedroom. Closing her eyes briefly, she willed herself to relax. This wasn't going to be much of a vacation.

Realizing she couldn't avoid the unavoidable, Eve tapped the engine button and the country music on the radio that had kept her company on her drive and the AC fan cut out. The silence enveloped her. Something akin to shame made her cheeks burn. She hoped her return to Hunters Ridge hadn't come too late.

Eve pushed open the door of her compact sedan, and the humid air assaulted her at the same time as the sharp shrill of cicadas. Had it always been this loud? Her heart beat in her ears as she crossed the yard. The wood planks creaked as she climbed the steps to her childhood home.

A commotion sounded on the other side of the door that made her pause and listen. Nostalgia, mixed with deep regret for all the time she had lost with her large Amish family, tightened like a band around her lungs, making it difficult to draw in a decent breath. Most of her siblings had grown and moved away to their own homes in Hunters Ridge or nearby Amish communities. However, her oldest brother, Thomas, and his children now occupied her former childhood home.

Mustering a strength that shouldn't have been this hard, considering they were her family, she finally knocked. The doorknob twisted and turned by some unseen hand.

"Let it alone, Jebediah." Her brother's deep, commanding voice reached out to her from an old memory, the harsh tone all too familiar. The door swung open, and a little boy who had merely been a speck in his mother's eye when Eve had fled Hunters Ridge slipped out onto the porch ahead of his father to inspect the stranger with narrowed eyes.

"Hello there." Eve smiled and pressed a hand to her favorite pink shirt that looked cute with her only pair of expensive jeans that she had so carefully selected from her limited wardrobe. She now realized how absolutely silly she had been. Anything other than a plain dress and bonnet would be an affront to her conservative, rule-following Amish brother. "I'm your—"

"Go inside." Her brother planted his hand on his son's head, gently turning him around and cutting short her introduction.

She swallowed hard and squared her shoulders. "Hello, Thomas." And then—unwilling to give him a chance to send her away—she added, "I came home to see *Mem*." His silence made her heart race. "Is she here? Or should I try the *dawdy haus*?" She could have tried the smaller house on the property, but she had wanted to announce her presence and face her biggest fear first in order to squash it.

But it seemed her brother wasn't going to make it easy. A muscle worked in his bearded jaw. A few strands of gray peppered his sandy brown beard despite him being only forty. Perhaps that was what being the father to six children did to a man. Thomas stepped fully onto the porch and pulled the door closed behind him. His expression softened for a fraction, as if he might be happy to see his long-lost sister, then his stern mask immediately settled back into place. "What are you doing here?"

"I came to visit Mother."

"Why now?" Suspicion sharpened his icy tone.

"It's time." Her niece Mercy had reached out to Eve to let her know Grandma Gerty was sick, but had begged Eve not to tell her father that she had called her.

Thomas seemed to be searching her face when the door opened behind him, first a fraction, then widely. Eve's heart exploded with affection and longing and shock. Her mother's round face had thinned and her bright eyes had hollowed. Leading with a cane she didn't need seven years ago, her mother stepped onto the porch. "Well, aren't you a sight for sore eyes." Her mother's voice cracked.

Tears immediately prickled the back of Eve's eyes. All the guilt and doubt and confusion at slipping away from Hunters Ridge in the middle of the night twisted like a garrote around her lungs.

"Hi, Mem." Eve stood rooted in place. A million questions clogged the back of her throat. Questions that would have to wait a hot second if she didn't want to betray Mercy's confidence.

"It's *gut* to see you." Her mother's lips quivered. Her papery-thin skin stretched across the bones of her thin face. Her faltering smile faded and she glared at her son. "Is this how you treat *die schweschder?*" Her mother lifted a shaky arm. "Come in. Abraham and Jebediah were about to play a board game with the girls, and I'm working on a quilt for Mercy's hope chest." Abraham had been a little guy when she left.

Eve dipped her head and stepped inside and immediately felt the weight of all the stares from strangers. Her family. Mercy sat stock-still on the floor with two toddlers, no doubt her youngest siblings. The worry creasing her eyes suggested she didn't trust Eve to keep her secret. That she had been the one who had tracked down Eve. Since Eve had left the Amish, she had been placed under the *Bann*. Perhaps if the family shunned her, she'd feel the pressure to return on bended knee.

Mercy had only been eleven when Eve had left. She and Mercy had a special bond, and little Hazel, now fourteen, had been forbidden from tagging along on their adventures in the woods. All these years later, Eve hardly recognized her nieces who had blossomed into beautiful young women. Only now, in their presence, did she feel the full impact of what she had missed out on. It was easy to dismiss her upbringing and avoid the feelings of neglect from being shunned when she had created a busy life in the outside world. Surely they had to understand that. She only wanted to see her *mem*. She wasn't looking for forgiveness.

Grandma Gerty, as her grandchildren, then her entire family had lovingly called her, sat down heavily in the rocking chair closest to the wood-burning fireplace that stood unused in the August summer heat. She ran her hand over the fabric stretched taut in a large rectangular frame that looked much like a table covered with a tablecloth. In another life, Eve would have sat down across from her and picked up a needle.

Not today.

Thomas remained standing a few feet away from Eve, as if blocking her entry farther into the house. Her mother looked up. "Children, this is your Aunt Eve." The older woman lifted a shaky hand to the younger children who probably never knew their aunt existed. Turned out Grace and Gabriel, the twins, were only eighteen months old. Jebediah, named after her grandfather, was six. The rest of the children—Abraham now twelve, Hazel, fourteen, and of course, Mercy, eighteen—had remembered their aunt from her plain days. At least the girls did. Abraham's memories might have faded since Eve had been gone for more years of his life than she had been here.

One of the babies toddled over to Eve and grabbed onto her pant leg, struggling to get a grip on the thick fabric of her jeans. She bent down and brushed her fingers across the child's hair, damp from a bath, no doubt. "Well hello there, little one."

"Mercy," Thomas called his oldest daughter with a hard edge to his voice, "please collect Grace."

Mercy jumped up and sheepishly met Eve's gaze. She took her little sister's hand and led her back over to where the toddler's twin played with wooden blocks.

"I came here to see mother," Eve said, feeling her cheeks heat at the reality of what her visit was going to look like with her brother demanding his children shun their evil aunt. Her best friend, Suze Oliver, who happened to be Carol's daughter, would get a kick out of the fact that her wholesome, teetotaler friend was considered the wild one back home.

A twinge of guilt softened Eve's frustration. Thomas probably shouldered much of the blame for her departure, even if only in his mind. When Eve was sixteen, their father had died suddenly, making Thomas the man of the house. He had moved into their childhood home with his young family.

Two short years later, Eve had jumped the fence in the middle of the night. She could only imagine how the tongues had wagged, blaming Thomas for not reining in his sister.

Jebediah, the six-year-old who had struggled to open the door when Eve arrived, had been hovering nearby and apparently worked up the nerve to speak. "You're our *aunt?*" The awe in his voice made her smile.

"Yes, I'm your *dat*'s sister."

Jebediah furrowed his little brow. "How come I never met you? Why are you wearing fancy clothes? Are you going to live with us?" The boy peppered her with questions, not allowing her room to answer.

Thomas planted his palm on his son's head. "It's time for your bath. Go on now."

Jebediah gave her a long look, as if memorizing her, or maybe trying to figure out the answers no one seemed to want to give him.

Eve tracked his movement toward the kitchen where Katy, her sister-in-law, hung back, as if avoiding her. Even though it came as no surprise, it hurt. She had loved her brother's wife like an older sister. Eve felt a smile pull on her lips, a sad smile at everything she had missed. "Hello, Katy."

Her sister-in-law held out her hand to draw in her son. "Come on, Jeb. Time to get you cleaned up."

Eve stood in the middle of the room, uncomfortable with all the eyes on her. The itchy feeling was reminiscent of the nagging suspicion she sometimes had when she was live on camera and suddenly wondered if her lunch was stuck in her teeth. It was hard to imagine this had once been her home.

"How did you find out about…" Thomas let his words trail off, another crack in his stern demeanor. He took a step closer and asked her in confidence, "You came to see *Mem*? How did you know?"

Eve cut a gaze to her mother who was leaning heavily on

the arm of the rocker, giving some quilting instructions to Hazel who had come to join her grandmother. Perhaps explaining the color choice or the best way to stitch. An immense feeling of nostalgia washed over her. Had it been that long ago that her mother—or her grandmother—had been teaching her the Amish fine arts? In Buffalo, she had taken up knitting, and her friends joked that she was like an old lady. What they didn't know was that she was trying to hang on to a piece of her childhood. Besides, the rhythmic motion and clacking of the knitting needles was soothing. A form of meditation.

"Eve?" Her brother pressed when she didn't answer.

"You of all people should know how gossipy Hunters Ridge is," Eve said, protecting her niece's secret. "*That's* how I found out that Mother's sick."

CHAPTER 2

Thomas must have sensed Eve wasn't going to give him the specifics on how she had ended up back in Hunters Ridge after a seven-year absence because he stopped pressing. She had owed her niece Mercy a debt of gratitude for letting her know about Grandma Gerty's recent health concerns. Eve would have never forgiven herself if her mother had died without her getting to say goodbye.

After a brief back-and-forth between Thomas and their mother, her brother had acquiesced to Eve staying in the *dawdy haus* for the night. Eve figured she'd take what she could get. She had grabbed her suitcase from the trunk of her car which she parked behind the barn, the same place one of her brothers had hid his pickup truck before he was baptized and settled down in the Amish community. Apparently Eve wasn't the only Reist with a wild streak in her. Unfortunately, the most rule-abiding sibling was the one she had to convince to allow her to stay longer than tonight.

Worst case, she'd rent a room at the Hunters Ridge Motel. But for now she'd sleep in the extra bedroom at her mother's small home on the same property. Perhaps in some tiny way Thomas was grateful someone else could shoulder the burden of their mother's care, not that he'd ever admit it.

Eve tossed her suitcase on the twin bed and felt a jolt of nostalgia at the sight of the familiar quilt of blues and greens made by her grandmother who once resided here. When Eve was a child, each of the grandchildren considered it a treat to sleep over at Grandma Sadie's. It was a fun reprieve from her own bustling family and the chance to be the center of attention for once. Her grandparents had long since passed and now Grandma Gerty lived in the house that stood across the lane from the main farmhouse.

Shaking away yet another memory—one of many that would be sure to haunt her during her stay—Eve changed into sweats and a T-shirt, made some tea, and settled in next to her mother on matching rocking chairs in the cozy sitting room.

Despite the August evening, her mother seemed chilled. "How are you, *Mem?*" Eve finally asked the question that had been at the forefront of her mind.

Her mother pressed her palms together and touched her index fingers to her pursed lips. "So, that's what brought you home?"

The accusation stung. But Eve couldn't deny it. "I was worried."

"Seems it finally caught up to me." The words sounded like something her mother had been long wanting to say, and her eyes grew red rimmed.

"Caught up with you?" Eve asked. The air felt cloying in the closed-up space.

"*Yah*, like Aunt Marian." The raw pain in her mother's voice was unlike anything Eve had ever heard. Her mother had always been strong, even when her father had died suddenly from a heart attack out in the fields. She had maintained a stiff upper lip, at least for her youngest daughter anyway.

"Breast cancer." It was a statement. The answer she already knew. Yet she wanted confirmation.

She nodded, her chin trembling.

"I'm sorry." Eve cleared the emotion from her throat. What else could she say? Even if some religious platitude would be welcomed, she'd feel like a hypocrite. She had left her faith behind years ago. Her Amish community had treated her too cruelly to continue their teachings, even in a different denomination. Add to that the fact that her mother had lost her older sister to breast cancer a year after Eve's father had died. How had *Gott* allowed that to happen?

Eve shoved her anger aside and asked, "Where are you going for treatment?"

"Thomas took me to see Dr. Gray."

"How long ago?"

Her mother twisted her lips, considering. "Maybe three months." Her tiny shrug accentuated her thin frame. Dr. Gray ran a small clinic in town. He was capable, but he certainly wasn't an oncologist.

"What did he say?" Eve found herself holding her breath.

"He encouraged me to go to Buffalo for a biopsy and treatment."

Eve blinked slowly. A spark of hope warmed her chest. "You haven't had a biopsy?"

Her mother turned her head and stared with wide eyes, a challenge lurking in their depths. "I don't need a biopsy. I can feel the lump."

Eve wrapped her hands around the arms of the chair, her fledgling optimism doused by icy cold dread. "You're not going to do anything?"

"I saw what Marian went through." Her mother slowly shook her head. A whisper of a memory flitted in Eve's brain and was gone. Her Aunt Marian's thin frame. Her gray pallor. Her weakness. "That's not for me. I have faith this is *Gott*'s plan."

Hot anger pulsed in Eve's ears. "You have to try something. You can't give up." She swallowed hard. "Aunt Marian died...what? Eight years ago? That's a lifetime when it comes to advancements in research and treatment."

Her mother seemed to flinch. "Why should I go through all that when I already know the end result? My poor sister." Her voice grew steely. "I invited you to stay here with me, but if you're going to harass me, you're going to have to leave."

Eve gasped at the harshness of her mother's comments. Would her mother really kick her out? She had always been the warm, loving parent. Her father and then her brother, after her *dat*'s death, had been the strict disciplinarians. The hollowness in Eve's stomach expanded and for a moment she wondered if she should have stayed away. What did her mother owe her when Eve hadn't even given her the consideration of a goodbye seven years ago?

"Okay, *Mem*," Eve said, primarily to placate her.

"Enough talk about me." There was a faraway quality to Grandma Gerty's voice. "I'd like to know what my baby girl has been up to since she ran away from home."

CHAPTER 3

"You were only in Buffalo…and you never came to visit?" Hurt made her mother's voice crack.

Eve frowned. "We both know that's not how this works when someone leaves the Amish."

A smile flickered at the corners of her mother's thin mouth. "How did you know I was sick?"

Eve hesitated a moment before saying, "Mercy." Grandma Gerty would never get her grandchildren in trouble, so Eve felt the secret was safe.

"Mercy?" Her mother's focus drifted toward the door. "How did she find you?"

"It's a funny story." Eve laughed, a mirthless sound. She suddenly felt like she was a teenager—before all her real problems started—trying to explain to her father why she hadn't done her morning chores because she got caught up in one of her books that was due back at the library the next day. "She saw me on television."

Gerty folded one hand over the other in her lap and tilted her head. "Television? What in the world?"

"Yeah, TV. Go figure." Perhaps if the Amish had allowed

modern conveniences, her family would have found her sooner. Eve had started out as an assistant producer shortly after college and had moved into the occasional fill-in, on-location reporter role over a year ago for the *AM Morning* show.

Her mother shivered.

"Are you cold?" Without waiting for an answer, Eve grabbed the quilt folded over the oak rack and placed it on her mother's lap. She remembered doing the same thing for her grandmother. Eve had an odd sense of déjà vu. Like no time had passed, yet eons had.

"Why would you be on TV? That's a silly place for her to find you, isn't it?" The crease in her brow made it clear she didn't understand.

Eve sniffed and closed her eyes briefly, trying to figure out where to begin. The Amish didn't like having photographs taken of themselves. According to Exodus, "Thou shall not make unto thee any graven image, or any likeness of anything that is in heaven above, or that is in the earth beneath, or that is in the water under the earth." Eve still could recite most of what she had been forced to memorize as a kid, even if she didn't follow the Amish's interpretation. The bishop certainly wouldn't be pleased to learn she was flaunting her disrespect for one of their tenets, and yet had the nerve to come home.

"I'm a reporter." She ran her hands up and down the smooth wood on the arms of the rocking chair. "I've done a lot of work behind the scenes preparing the news, but more recently I've been getting time on camera. And next month, I'll be on the morning broadcast daily. It's a show called *AM Morning*." Strange how her career was unfolding, especially because her passion was writing. Yet her degree in journalism had landed her in broadcasting. And since she needed to pay the rent, she couldn't say no to a great job.

"How did Mercy happen to see you?" Her mother glanced over with hooded eyelids. She was obviously tired. Then she shook her head. "Her father keeps her close, but I know as well as anyone how the youths find ways to get around the rules."

Another time Eve might have felt the zing of the comment, but right now she was happy to have this conversation at all. "I don't want her to get into trouble."

Grandma Gerty waved her hand, and Eve took that as acceptance.

"She said she saw me on television at a friend's house and she called the station. They reached out to me. It took some coordinating before we actually talked because Mercy doesn't have a phone."

"Thomas has one in that small shed where he does some business."

Eve nodded. "She was afraid Thomas would be upset with her."

"Hmmm." Her mother seemed to consider this. "That is true." She tapped on the arm of the rocker with her index finger. "How long before you have to get back to your work?" The question was asked around a yawn.

"I have two weeks of vacation." She could probably extend it to a month if she had to. Eve hoped that was enough time to convince her mother to go to Buffalo for further tests and treatment if necessary.

"Do you plan to stay in Hunters Ridge for the duration?" Her mother's tone was ripe with hope.

"That's my plan, but I suppose I'll have to work on Thomas."

Her mother's forehead wrinkled. "He feels the weight of raising *gut* children."

The retort that she was his sister, not his daughter, died on her lips. "I'd like to take you to Buffalo for a consultation."

Her mother shifted slightly forward in the rocking chair and when it seemed like too much effort, she leaned back. "I'm not...*Neh...*" She shook her head to emphasize her point.

Eve reached out and covered her mother's hand. "We don't have to discuss it tonight. You're tired."

Grandma Gerty turned her hand over so that their palms were touching, and her mother squeezed her hand, albeit weakly. "I'm happy you're home."

They sat in companionable silence for a few moments, then her mother scooted to the edge of her chair. She waved Eve off again when she tried to help her mother stand.

"Hand me my cane." The frustration in Mem's voice was palpable.

Eve righted the cane that had fallen behind the chair and handed it to her. Grandma Gerty planted the cane and stood, a subtle light of triumph in her eyes, as if to say, *See, I got it!*

"Do you have everything you need, *Mem*?" Eve asked, forcing herself to remain seated when the urge to assist her mother was strong.

The woman she loved most in the world paused at her bedroom door to the right of the sitting area and shifted to look at her youngest daughter. "I'm fine."

Her brow twitched and Eve's heart ached. She didn't bother to ask about the pain because she already knew the answer. The same as the one she had just muttered—*I'm fine.* How long had Grandma Gerty been swallowing her pain? Being the martyr? The cold feeling of dread that she had been battling all day swirled in Eve's gut.

"Do you still like a big breakfast?" her mother asked, snapping Eve out of her spiraling thoughts.

Eve was lucky if she guzzled a cup of coffee on the early morning drive to work. "You don't have to go to any trouble for me."

"You're not trouble. How about I make apple pancakes?

Katy picked up some beautiful apples from the farmers market in town the other day. There's a bushel in the pantry."

Eve forced a watery smile. "Sounds wonderful."

Her mother took a step back and stifled a yawn. *"Guten nacht."*

"Night, *Mem.*"

Eve pushed off the rocker and peeked out the window across the field toward her brother's house. The soft glow of a kerosene lamp filtered out from her old bedroom window, the one Mercy now occupied. Eve turned away and slipped into the spare bedroom and closed the door with a quiet click. She slid her laptop from the outside sleeve of her suitcase. She sat down on the familiar quilt and already felt guilt nagging at her, remorse for breaking rules that no longer applied to her.

Eve propped up the single thin pillow and leaned back, resting against the pine headboard. She dragged a hand through her hair as she waited for her laptop to boot up. She remembered the first time she had gotten her hair cut. Eighteen inches of hair fastened together for donation to some charity that Annie Yutzy, the woman who helped her transition to the outside world, had arranged. It had seemed like a nice gesture. The new style had suddenly made her feel lighter. Free. The blonde highlights had felt like another act of rebellion, of shedding the past. Right now she probably had enough hair to pull it into a ponytail and twist it into a small bun, not that she planned to.

She tugged on the collar of her T-shirt in the warm room. She slipped off the bed and opened the window a fraction. The high shrill of the cicadas swept into the room on the sweet scent of the summer night air. She lifted the laptop and pulled it into her lap and tried to get comfortable on the twin bed. She connected to a probably not very reliable hotspot on her cell phone. After a few tries, she opened her blog.

Writing had always been her outlet. She had started the anonymous blog years ago while still in college, but had let it lapse after graduation. For some reason, being back in Hunters Ridge made her long to share her feelings. To talk into the void. And maybe someone like her, who had left her Amish family behind, was on the other end, reading. Perhaps they'd both feel a little better.

She began typing.

It's been a long time since I've posted on here.

She smiled to herself, a bit sadly, at the thought that anyone cared what she had to say, or that she had been absent for so long. Back when she first started the blog, she'd been buoyed by some consistent commenters who seemed to be looking for advice, or assurances that they had made the right decision. The darkest time for Eve had been immediately after she left home. The doubts had weighed on her. She had wanted to be a voice of reassurance for other lost souls. She placed her fingers on the keyboard and began to type in the casual way she always did on her blog, as if she was holding a conversation over coffee.

I guess it's easy to ignore your past when you're busy planning your future. Or maybe my true problem was being so absorbed in my day-to-day life—survival—that I failed to consider either. Today, my past has made itself known in no uncertain terms. For the first time since I snuck out of my childhood home in the middle of the night, I have returned. To my Amish home. I won't say where because I've never gotten into specifics. I suppose that's to protect my family. To protect me. I have so many thoughts as I get ready to go to sleep—yes, I know, I probably shouldn't be using a laptop in my mem's home—but I keep circling back to the same thing: I spent so much time planning to leave, I didn't give much thought to what it would be like to return.

Can you ever go home?

Eve ran her hand over the stitching on the quilt made by

her grandmother's hand. Eve had picked out the colors when she was fourteen. The quilt had been for her hope chest. But when she left, she hadn't taken the chest or much hope. She had been all but defeated. She often lamented losing all the things she had accumulated over the years when she had been planning to establish her own Amish home. Thomas had thrown out her personal items and repurposed things—like this quilt.

Her mind drifted to the journals she had kept as a young girl. She had been drawn to the empty blank pages in the stationery store in town. She bought one with the money she had saved from the sale of her homemade pies to the diner. Most nights, she wrote down her thoughts and hid it deep in her hope chest for fear she'd be punished.

The cursor blinked on the glowing laptop screen in the darkened room. Writing an anonymous blog was freeing. She could unburden herself. Her gaze drifted to the window and her hollowed-out reflection stared back at her. The fine hairs on the back of her neck prickled to life, the way they did when she was doing a live report, as if someone was watching her. Someone other than the viewers at home. It didn't help that an overzealous fan had been leaving her creepy gifts and notes, the frequency of which had ramped up recently. But no one knew Evelyn Phoenix—the name she used on air and in her new life in Buffalo—was Eve Reist, the quiet girl who had grown up in an Amish family. She was safe here. At least from unhinged viewers. She couldn't speak about the enemies she had made before she left Hunters Ridge.

Eve set the laptop aside and slid out of bed and yanked the roller shade down. Unsurprisingly, it shot back up with a loud thwack. Heart racing, she glanced toward her closed bedroom door. Hopefully her mother hadn't been disturbed. Eve stretched up and pulled the edge of the blind, freezing and staring past her own reflection to the wide yard that flowed into the swaying cornfields and the barn.

A million memories assaulted her. She massaged her temple. Drawing in a calm breath, she let it out slowly. She climbed back into bed and grabbed her laptop and read her words.

Can you ever go home?

Eve poised her fingers over the keyboard.

I've been gone from the Amish community for seven years. But now that I'm here, it feels like yesterday. And a hundred years. Both no time and an eternity. I feel like the person I was, growing up Amish, and the person I became in the outside world are fighting for attention. I thought I had put the Amish girl away forever. But she's still here. And so am I.

Eve drummed her fingers lightly on the edge of her laptop. The words that normally allowed her to put her thoughts in order didn't come. She saved a draft of her blog. Maybe she no longer needed to share. Maybe the act of writing was therapy enough.

CHAPTER 4

It seemed to take forever for Eve to drift off to sleep. Her nerves were on fire. Between feeling like she was straddling two worlds, and her mother's health, she couldn't shut off her brain. She wasn't sure if she had fallen completely asleep or if she had been lying awake when a strange noise crept into her subconscious. Unspecified fear flitted across her skin, making her feel uneasy. She opened her eyes and blinked. The complete darkness was suffocating. Her pulse roared in her ears, the only sound in the silence.

Maybe she imagined it.

Screech...

The sound came again and the fine hairs on the back of her neck prickled to life. She flipped back the quilt and sat up. Her bare feet hit the cold hardwood floor. She had left the window open a crack. The bedroom was on the ground floor. If she had been in her apartment in the city, she would have never been so careless. But she wasn't in her apartment. She was in her mother's house. In Hunters Ridge. Maybe the branches from the large oak tree were raking against the outside wall.

Her mouth having gone dry, she crossed the small space and pulled back the corner of the blind. A shadowlike form moved across the field in awkward lumbering movements, as if they were running hunched over in the moonless night. The person seemed to stop, then redirect, moving toward the front of her house. Her panic spiked. Eve ran to get her cell phone. She bashed her thigh on the nightstand. She switched on the flashlight app and froze. Then frantically turned it off. She didn't want to make herself a target.

Had she or her mother locked the door? Had an overzealous fan from Buffalo tracked her down here? Her brain clicked through all her self-defense training. What should she do next?

She shook her head and moved back toward the window and peeked out. Were her past experiences with a creepy viewer clouding her judgment? Making her too quick to think the worst? She was in Hunters Ridge, for goodness' sake. The clouds had parted, revealing the moon and an empty field. The cornstalks swayed in the breeze.

I saw someone in the yard. I didn't imagine that.

Fear heated her cheeks. The window rumbled in its frame as she slid it shut, then turned the lock. She rushed through the small *dawdy haus* to check the front door. The Amish lived mostly unafraid out in the country, but she now realized the flimsy lock on the handle probably wouldn't withstand a swift kick. Eve ran the back of her hand across her neck. When had she become so jaded? So paranoid? During her self-defense classes when the instructor saw to it that she recognized the danger in any situation.

Not wanting to waste time or risk the safety of her family, she hurriedly called 911 and told them there was a trespasser on the property. After giving them her address she hung up, even though they asked her to stay on the line. She needed to be quiet. With a trembling hand, she reached out and turned the small lock on the handle and opened the door. A warm summer breeze flowed in. Muffled angry voices sounded from across the yard. She squinted and could only make out their forms.

Was it her niece? Had the person come looking for Mercy and accidentally found Eve's bedroom window instead? She stepped back into the shadows. It wasn't unusual for the youths to sneak out at night to hang with their girlfriends, but she didn't get the sense that Mercy had a boyfriend. In the few conversations Eve had with her, she only referred to her friends—the ones who had snuck to nearby Fredonia in a friend's car where she happened to see her aunt on TV. She had assumed her niece was with a bunch of girls. Maybe Eve hadn't asked the right questions. Today, Mercy seemed demure and obedient in the presence of her father, not the type of teen who would be sneaking out with a boy.

But it wouldn't be unusual for a young Amish woman to be keeping secrets. Like a special friend who snuck by the farm to pay a late-night visit.

Eve suddenly questioned her rash decision to dial 911.

She considered slipping back into the house and calling the sheriff's department to tell them to forget it, that she had made a mistake, but something compelled her to stand in the shadows for a fraction of a moment longer.

Their discussion had grown louder. A lovers' quarrel? Eve's own boyfriend, before she finally dumped him, had been possessive. And the Amish man who everyone had expected her to marry had been a real piece of work, too. She stopped thoughts of Aaron Brenneman before they could take root.

The woman stepped away from the main farmhouse, and Eve recognized her definitively as her niece. Something in

Mercy's body language gave Eve pause. Eve silently prayed she'd slip inside and not give the guy the time of day. If only someone had given her advice to stand up for herself when she was a young girl.

The Amish community wasn't exactly a bedrock for women's rights.

"Just leave, buddy," Eve muttered. "Just leave."

"Lookie here." A low, menacing whisper sounded from around the side of her porch, sending a new wave of panic rolling over her. An unforgettable voice. *Aaron Brenneman.*

Eve stepped back and slammed the heel of her bare foot into the closed door behind her. As if the mere thought of the jerk had conjured him out of the night. Pinpricks washed over her skin. She was seventeen again. Frozen in place. Trapped.

Aaron stumbled up the porch steps. Eve wrapped her hand around the doorknob, ready to retreat. But she wasn't seventeen anymore. She squared her shoulders. "You need to leave." Her tone held a razor-sharp edge that his smug face barely registered. She didn't bother to ask him why he was here. She didn't care.

Yet she knew.

She had been gone seven years, but people didn't forget.

He tilted his head. She couldn't see his expression in the shadows, but she had seen the look of his beady eyes, the snarl on his lips, the scent of stale beer on his breath before. From the foul smell rolling off him, he had graduated to something harder. "Go away, Aaron. Get out of here."

"I'm not going anywhere." He slurred his words and let his gaze rake down the length of her.

She was dressed modestly in her sweatpants and T-shirt, but she had to fight the urge to cross her arms over her chest. "What do you want?" she asked, grinding out her words.

"You're not welcome here. Not anymore."

"Leave." A ripple of dread washed over her, but she stood her ground.

"I'm highly respected in Hunters Ridge." His slack jaw made his speech sound sloppy.

Eve jerked her head back and anger stiffened her spine. "Highly respected, huh?" She balled her fist, but knew firsthand how ineffective her punches were against his broad chest. "Is that why you're out here taunting me? Drunk? Who's harassing my niece?"

"No one's harassing your niece." There was a mocking quality to his voice. He planted his hand against the frame of the door next to her head and lowered his face to within inches of hers.

She ducked under his arm and stepped off the small porch, giving herself room to get away. She'd never allow herself to be trapped by him. Not again. He took a few awkward steps and caught the railing to steady himself.

Eve's gaze drifted briefly across the way toward her niece and the stranger. Aaron's drunken display had drawn their attention.

Mercy broke free and ran toward Eve, the stranger a few feet behind her. "I'm sorry, Aunt Eve." Then to Aaron, "You're going to wake up my family."

"We won't. We're leaving," the other man who was apparently Roy said. He jumped up on the porch and shoved Aaron toward the steps. "Come on. I told you this was a bad idea."

Aaron ran a hand roughly over his face as if trying to sober up. "I'm respected around here and you better keep your mouth shut," he said before stumbling down the steps. Roy muttered something Eve couldn't make out as he kept close tabs on Aaron as they made their way toward the road.

Anger heated Eve's face and she bit back a response she'd most likely regret. When she had left Hunters Ridge seven years ago, it had been to get away from Aaron. She had no intention of revisiting her past.

"See you at the bonfire," Roy hollered over his shoulder to Mercy. Eve suspected they had a car parked somewhere nearby because Aaron was in no condition to walk far.

"I'm so sorry," Mercy said, keeping her voice low. "I couldn't get him to leave."

"I don't understand why they were here." Eve had never shared her story with Mercy. Her niece was only a little girl when it all happened. And she was too young for town gossip.

The look in Mercy's eyes made her seem mature beyond her years.

"Who was that other man?" Eve asked.

"Roy Brenneman."

Brenneman. "What relationship is he to Aaron?"

"They're cousins."

Eve crossed her arms tightly over her chest. "Aaron is bad news." She stopped short, unwilling to revisit that horrible night a few weeks before she had left town. Who was she kidding? She relived that night on a regular basis. That was why she filled her days with work. Easier to not think about the past when she was preoccupied with the present.

Mercy's lips twitched. "I didn't know he was going to bother you. I swear."

"You told them I was here?" She searched her niece's face in the heavy shadows.

"*Neh, neh*...I was with Roy when I first saw you on the news. I was so surprised to see you. I couldn't believe it. We talked about it all the way home from Fredonia. I had no idea he'd tell his cousin about you. I mean, why would he?"

Eve was weighing what she wanted to share about Aaron Brenneman when the blue and red lights of a patrol car turned up the lane. She muttered her displeasure under her breath.

Mercy's hands flew to her mouth. "*Dat's* going to kill me."

Eve squared her shoulders. "Go in. I'll handle this. I'm the one who called the sheriff's department."

"Why would you do that?" The disbelief in Mercy's tone made Eve's heart ache. She had been home for only a few hours, and if she had any hopes of reconciling with her niece, she had already blown it.

"I didn't…I…I'm sorry." Eve ran a hand over her hair and glanced down at her T-shirt and sweatpants and bare feet. "Let me handle this. It's my fault they're here."

Mercy took a step back. "Are you sure?" A sliver of hope that she'd avoid the wrath of her father tinged her voice and restored a glimmer of faith that maybe she could patch her relationship with her niece.

Reflexively, Eve's stomach clenched. She had hated those days of always being afraid of doing the wrong thing. She forced a smile. "Yes, go. I'm already on the naughty list. There's nothing your father can do to me." Except kick her out when she wanted to be nearby to take care of her mother.

Mercy had spun around to leave when the deputy got out of his patrol car. "Everyone okay here? Someone reported a trespasser."

"We're fine. I'm the one who called 911," Eve said, then to Mercy, "Go on in before your parents wake up."

The deputy turned toward Eve, his face shadowed by his hat in the darkness. "I take it the trespasser is gone?"

"Yeah." She stepped off the porch, the grass cool on her bare feet, and strolled over to him. He moved into the beam from his headlights and her heart dropped. Awareness heated every inch of her body, and she had to pause to collect herself before his name floated out on a quiet whisper. "Dylan."

He tilted his head and recognition made him smile. "Eve. Eve Reist?" His eyes traveled the length of her and then returned to her face. "Is that… You're back?" Confusion laced his tone.

Emotions she couldn't quite get her head or heart wrapped around made it difficult to speak. She held up her palms and forced a playful tone. "I am."

CHAPTER 5

*E*ve Reist, the pretty Amish girl he had once known, stepped out of the darkness—out of his past—into the beam of light from the headlights of his patrol car. Her presence jolted him back to the days when he was working his way through college at the local theater, and she had come in to catch whatever movie happened to be playing. When it was quiet, he'd sneak in and join her in the back row. They innocently connected over free buttered popcorn and Milk Duds, her favorite. Prior to getting to know her, the Amish in his hometown had always seemed to be "other."

A million questions flooded his brain, but now was not the time. He was here in an official capacity. Eve had called the sheriff's department. "What happened out here?" His gaze drifted toward the house where the young Amish girl had retreated. "Everyone okay?"

"Yes, we're fine. I sent my niece inside so she wouldn't get in trouble with her father."

She threaded her fingers and twisted her hands, much like she'd done at the back of the theater when they'd discussed their future plans. Their individual future plans.

She had always seemed conflicted. And foolishly he'd thought maybe he had been the reason.

"Some drunk guy was harassing us," she continued. "But he's gone. We're fine."

"Do you want to file a report?" He suspected this question was pointless. Most Amish wanted to stay separate. The fact that he had been called to this location had surprised even dispatch. Now it made sense—Eve had dialed the phone. As far as he knew, she hadn't been part of the Amish community since she had left, which didn't explain what she was doing here. With her arms tightly wrapped around her midsection, dressed in a T-shirt, and her painted toenails sticking out from her oversize sweatpants, she looked like any one of the young women he had occasionally dated. Actually, she was prettier than most, or perhaps he was biased. Her hair seemed lighter than it had been years ago and hung loose around her shoulders. Her features had matured, but she was unmistakably the shy Amish friend from his past.

Eve warily looked at the house. "It's probably best if I don't file a report."

Dylan wanted an explanation. Who was she trying to protect? They both shifted at the sound of another vehicle approaching. A second patrol car pulled up behind his. The deputy climbed out and nodded in his direction.

"Slow night." Caitlin smiled in a disarming way. She looked at Eve with curiosity and extended her hand. "Deputy Caitlin Flagler."

"Eve..." She seemed to pause a moment, as if she was going to say something else, then continued more confidently. "Eve Reist. I'm sorry to cause all this commotion. I overreacted." She shifted and planted one bare foot on top of the other, as if trying to keep her feet warm. "My niece had some drunk Amish guy follow her home from Sunday singing. But everything is fine now." She pointed at the small building behind her. "I'm visiting and I suppose I forgot how rowdy these youths can get." He wasn't buying her feigned confusion for a second. Something else was going on here.

"How did they leave here?" Dylan asked.

"They headed toward the road on foot. Perhaps they had a car parked somewhere close by."

"Do you know their names?" Caitlin asked.

Eve pressed her lips together. "I'd rather let it be."

"If they were drunk and harassing your niece, why are you trying to protect them?" Caitlin had always been a no-nonsense deputy.

"Roy and Aaron Brenneman. They're cousins." Eve kept flicking her gaze toward the house, apparently afraid someone would come out.

"Brenneman? What relationship to the bishop?" Dylan asked. The ties were strong in the small Amish community.

"Grandsons," Eve answered.

"I need to get a statement from your niece, too," Dylan said.

"I'd rather you kept her out of it. I only came back today, and I'd like to build some trust with her." Eve's frown was caught in the shadows thrown off from the lights on the patrol cars. "I just met Roy, but I have a history with Aaron. This isn't the first time he's gotten drunk and harassed me. He must have heard I was in town and decided to pay me a visit." She shook her head, as if dismissing something more sinister. "Just a drunk ex, I guess." She tried to sound casual, but she wasn't pulling it off.

"What am I missing here?" Caitlin asked the question on Dylan's mind.

Eve studied her feet. "Nothing, they were just being drunk fools. I chased them off. I shouldn't have been so quick to dial 911. Sorry for wasting your time."

Caitlin lifted her hands and took a few steps backward.

"That's our job." She spun on her heel. "I'm going to head out and see if I find anyone behind the wheel of a car who shouldn't be there."

Eve looked like she wanted to protest.

"Thanks, deputy," Dylan said. Then he turned toward Eve. "How long do you plan to stay in Hunters Ridge?" It had been seven years since they used to hang out at the theater, but standing in front of her now took him right back. Her weary smile. Her flawless skin. Her soft voice. But he still couldn't get over her *Englisch* appearance.

"I'm not sure." Her voice cracked. "My mother is sick. I came for a visit." She glanced toward the small house on the property. He had lived his whole life in Hunters Ridge and knew that the Amish often had what they called a *dawdy haus* for the grandparents to live in. "My brother lives in the main house now," she said, as if reading his mind.

"I'm sorry about your mother. Is there anything I can do?"

Eve shook her head. "No, thanks." She crossed her arms over her chest and frowned. "I'm sorry I wasted your time," she repeated.

"Like Deputy Flagler said, it's my job."

"Well, I appreciate it, but we're fine." She pointed at the door with her thumb. "I better go in. Good night."

"Night." Dylan stepped out of the headlights and into the darkness. He slowed, then turned back around and called to her. She paused on the porch and he pulled a business card from his pocket and handed it to her. "If you need anything, or want to grab coffee sometime while you're here, give me a call."

The shadows kept him from seeing her face, but he imagined her shy, pretty smile as she accepted the card. "I'm only in town to make sure my mother gets proper care," she said softly, as if it pained her somehow.

"Of course." Dylan tipped his hat and opened his car door.

An annoying *ding-ding-ding* floated out into the still night air. He waved, acting casual. "It was nice seeing you. Take care."

He climbed behind the wheel of his cruiser, unable to shake the shock from seeing Eve Reist again. His gut tightened at how easily she had brushed him off.

Why should he expect otherwise? Eve had shown him who she was seven years ago when she left Hunters Ridge without so much as a goodbye.

CHAPTER 6

The next morning Eve woke up and her eyes felt gritty from lack of sleep. She lay in her twin bed for a moment to collect herself before facing the day. Facing Thomas. There was no way he'd missed the goings-on outside his own front door late last night. What she didn't understand was why he didn't confront her then. It would have been a perfect opportunity to send her packing if that's what he wanted to do.

Eve plumped up her pillow and tried to relax her body and mind, but the buzz of nerves made her stomach ache. The first night in Hunters Ridge and her past had come roaring back in full force. Awful Aaron Brenneman, the man who had single-handedly changed the course of her life, had found her. *Already.* Her niece had innocently led him to her door. Was it merely a coincidence that his cousin Roy was friends with Mercy?

Eve dismissed the idea that Mercy and Roy's relationship was anything but genuine. It was a small town where everyone knew everyone else. That was all. And had Eve really thought Aaron wouldn't get wind of her return? *No,* but she didn't think it would happen this quickly. And certainly not in such dramatic fashion.

And to see Dylan Kimble again. Handsome, sweet Dylan. Forbidden, *Englisch* Dylan. Her first—and only—teenage crush. When he initially sat down next to her in the back of the theater all those years ago, Eve feared she had done something wrong. Then when he started making small talk, she'd suspected he had felt sorry for her sitting all alone. Then over the course of a few movies, their friendship blossomed over shared snacks and movie lines.

Thankfully, there was a movie screen to distract her from his dark brown eyes that seemed to look deep into her soul when they locked eyes. Eve closed her eyes and let the memory wash over her as she snuggled under the covers to delay the start of her day. Oh, and his hair. She loved the stylish cut, shorter on the sides and longer on the top, so different from the blunt cuts of the Amish guys in her life. When she discovered he was a few years older than she was and in college, she had become smitten. He had to have seen that, but he never called her out on it. Why had he bothered with a plain Amish girl at all? She had never learned the answer, but suspected it had something to do with killing time during his long work shift at the quiet theater.

Eve tucked her nose under the quilt, smelling the familiar laundry detergent her mother used. Her relationship with Dylan had been harmless because he was so far out of her league—a term she learned after leaving the Amish. Yet they often talked long after the movie ended and the theater emptied out. He'd sweep up the stray popcorn and she'd hold the dustpan. They shared the most random things about each other. Her heart warmed at the memory.

Eve stretched her arm out from under the quilt and slid Dylan's business card off her bedside table—one her grandfather had handcrafted—and held it up in the early morning light filtering in around the thin white blind. She couldn't help but think of her own apartment in Buffalo, simple because she hadn't been making the big money yet. But she had purposely decorated with color and flair, something missing in her childhood home. Missing in her mother's smaller space now, too. Back home, Eve had thick purple room-darkening shades. She had recently started looking at real estate—small homes—now that she had that big promotion on the *AM Morning* show. She'd finally have steady hours, even if they were at the crack of dawn.

Butterflies flitted in her stomach at the thought. Her life and career in Buffalo seemed like a world away. Her busy days seemed to be moving in a positive direction until she got that phone call from Mercy. Everything had come to a screeching halt, and now all the good things in her life had hues of gray. How would she deal with the guilt if her mother died? Eve had wasted so much time away.

Eve flipped Dylan's business card over in her hand. *Speaking of wasting time.* She felt a compulsion to reach out to him. To see what he had been up to. To see if life had turned out like he had planned. He had talked about moving to a bigger city after college graduation. Becoming a lawyer. So, it had been doubly shocking to find he was working as a sheriff's deputy in town.

A flicker of disappointment tamped down her butterflies. Was he married? Did he have children? Surely he wouldn't be inviting her for coffee if he had a wife?

He was just doing his job. Being nice. He was always so, so nice.

She set the business card down. Her priority was her mother's care, not her past in Hunters Ridge. Her future was in Buffalo. At least for now. Her job could take her to bigger markets. Growing up with such deep roots in Hunters Ridge made the thought of having no permanent home both exciting and terrifying.

Realizing she couldn't avoid the long day ahead, she slipped out of bed wearing her sweatpants and T-shirt from last night. The bottoms of her feet were dirty. She made coffee in the French press. With her mug in hand, she stood outside her mother's bedroom door and peered through the small opening, reassured by her mother's measured breathing. What if she had died before Eve had been able to come home to say goodbye? Unease whispered across the back of her neck. Hadn't that always been a possibility? Perhaps the abstract idea of it never felt real. Her mother was still young by anyone's standards. She was supposed to have more years. A *lot* more years.

Eve took another sip of her coffee, at once needing the caffeine and realizing it was doing nothing for her nerves. One cup. That was all she'd have. She stuffed her feet into her sneakers, crunching the backs, and shuffled outside and sat down in the solitary rocker on the small porch. Across the way, her brother's house had a wide porch with rockers and a swing. That was her favorite spot growing up, but now she didn't feel welcome to use it. Her brother had begrudgingly accepted her presence in her mother's home. And only for the night.

She took a sip of her coffee and inhaled the rich aroma. She had missed the simple coffee, having acquired a taste for fancy espressos and such at the coffeehouses in Buffalo. She had also missed the quiet, easy start to a day. Unlike her early mornings before dawn, reporting from some crash site, or on slower news days when they'd let her guest host. She supposed that had been the opportunity that led to her current promotion.

A billow of steam drifted from the surface of the coffee. She had always loved early morning before the sun warmed the land. Something about the crispness of it. And more than summer, she loved autumn. Too bad she wouldn't still be here then. She wished she had savored her last autumn in Hunters Ridge.

Across the way, the screen door screeched open and she looked up. Her brother stepped out onto the porch, and a new shot of adrenaline surged through her veins. From this distance she couldn't make out his expression, but his body language said all she needed to know. She took a sip to fortify herself against the impending confrontation.

She tucked in her chin and tracked her brother's movements across the field. It reminded her of all the times a curious bystander wandered over to her and her cameraman to ask what they were doing, usually with an edge of annoyance. She often wondered if journalists had always been considered the enemy or if this was a more recent development. Although she was apprehensive about facing her brother this morning, she took comfort in knowing he was a known commodity, and she wasn't in any serious jeopardy—unless she counted getting asked to leave his property.

Eve forced herself to remain seated as her brother approached. Thomas Reist had taken over the family farm when their father died. Eve had only been sixteen. Since he was fifteen years her senior, he had also assumed a paternal role, no doubt taking personal offense at her every transgression. He had taken heat from the elders of the church regarding her behavior, and she imagined it didn't stop after she left. People tended to enjoy reminding others of their shortcomings.

Poor Mercy would be paying for Eve's wrongdoings since her brother undoubtedly wouldn't allow his oldest daughter to make him look like a fool in the eyes of the elders. Not again.

When Thomas reached the railing-less porch, he planted his boot on the bottom step and rested one elbow on his thigh. A muscle ticked in his jaw and she waited for him to speak. In a way, she felt like a petulant child daring him to make the first move in a world where her brother was no longer in charge of her.

Thomas pushed his straw hat up on his forehead and stared at her with his piercing dark eyes. "You are a guest in my home. You are not going to stir things up again."

The accusation that she had been causing a commotion was a familiar punch to the gut. "I'm not looking for trouble. I..." She chose her words carefully, unwilling to throw Mercy under the bus. "I thought I saw a trespasser on the property and called the sheriff's department. Perhaps it was an overreaction. For that, I'm sorry."

"Did you see them?" Thomas lifted an eyebrow and she suspected a trap.

"Mercy's allowed to meet her friends at the Sunday singing, right? I heard her getting dropped off. It was my mistake."

Her brother seemed to consider this for a moment. "Is there something you're not telling me?"

Eve's shoulders sagged. "Thomas, please. I'm here for Mother. That's all."

He narrowed his gaze, perhaps realizing she wasn't going to give him more information. "I am not going to be gossiped about."

A flush of anger heated her face. She rested her forearms on her thighs, mirroring his posture. The rocker tipped forward. She held the coffee mug by the rim casually between her knees. "It's no fun to be the subject of gossip, is it?" She lifted a defiant eyebrow.

"I am a respected member of this community."

She leaned back and took a sip of her coffee. As the black liquid hit her gut she felt queasy, but she didn't show it. She was not sixteen. Or eighteen, for that matter. She was twenty-five and independent. She had interviewed far more intimidating people in her line of work, and she wasn't going to let her own brother scare her. "I didn't deserve to be the subject of gossip either, and I don't remember you coming to my defense." There, she had said it. The fury that had been building up since she had run away in the middle of the night rushed out of her mouth in a simple, calm statement.

Thomas pushed off his thigh and straightened. "I have no interest in reliving the mess from years ago. You made your choice. You left. I'm allowing you to visit *Mem* as a courtesy. Remember that."

Eve stood and tossed the contents of her cup onto the dewy grass. "I'm going to make sure Mother gets the best care." She ground out the words hoping she didn't sound as perturbed as she felt. She would not give her brother the satisfaction.

"*Gott* has a plan. Mem doesn't want to go for a consultation in Buffalo. You're doing this to ease your own conscience. You're as selfish as ever."

Emotion made it hard to talk. He gave voice to her precise fears. Acceptance of the inevitable was not okay. "*Gott*'s plan? Giving up that easily? We don't even know what she's dealing with. She hasn't had a biopsy." She found herself practically shouting in frustration.

Thomas's face grew red. "Do not call my faith into question."

Eve blinked slowly and lowered her voice. "God has given some very smart doctors better treatment options since Aunt Marian died. She doesn't have to accept this. Whatever it might be. Maybe it's early stage. Maybe it's not cancer." She tossed the last statement out, but considering the family history, she didn't put much hope in that kind of good news.

"Do you mean *you* don't have to accept this?" His gravelly voice grated across her last nerve.

Eve narrowed her gaze and bit her lip. What could she say

anyway? She couldn't wear out the welcome mat. If she already hadn't.

Just when she thought—hoped—he was going to walk away, he said, "I know you're hiding something."

Emboldened by the experience of living her life out from under the strict rules of the *Ordnung*, Eve asked, "Why do you care what I have to say now when you wouldn't listen to me before I left?"

"I'm not talking about years ago." Her brother's lips thinned, reminding her of his stubborn streak. "I want to know what was going on outside my door last night."

Eve tilted her head and shrugged, a casual gesture that hid the rage boiling underneath. She reached behind her and twisted the doorknob with a trembling hand. "When it comes to our relationship, Thomas, everything has to do with what happened all those years ago."

Eve slipped into the house and closed the door with a quiet click—when in reality she wanted to slam the door—and pressed her forehead against it, relishing the cool feel of the wood.

CHAPTER 7

*E*ve's heart beat wildly in her chest after the confrontation with her brother. She'd had this argument in her head with him, but this was the first time she had given voice to it. Unremarkably, it did nothing to bring her peace. She'd have to catch Mercy alone later to talk. The fact that her niece was friends with Aaron's cousin wasn't unusual in a small town, but something about the whole situation felt too convenient. Or maybe Eve's paranoia had roared back with her return. Determined to keep it together, she pushed away from the door and was surprised to find her mother watching her, a cheerless smile on her pale face.

Eve was struck anew with how much Grandma Gerty had aged in the past seven years and it made her sad. Remorseful, all over again, that she had lost this time with her. Uncertain if their mother had overheard the argument on the porch, Eve readied her apology.

But her mother spoke first, her voice weak from age, from sickness, maybe both. "Your brother is a *gut* man."

His need to be seen as good blinds him sometimes to what is right. What is just. Instead of saying any of that, Eve muttered,

"We'll never see eye to eye." She forced a smile. "What should I cook?" she added, changing the subject.

Her mother planted her heavy cane on the hardwood floor and shuffled over to the kitchen area and stretched to grab a frying pan. "I believe I promised *you* breakfast."

The weight on Eve's chest eased at the familiarity of watching her mother in the kitchen. "I can help."

"I know, but I'd like to do this for you." She flicked on the flame to the gas stove, then turned to face her daughter. "Can you make the coffee? I didn't sleep well."

"Of course." Eve quickly went about making fresh coffee for her mother, wondering if she had overheard that commotion last night, too. Her heart sank. If Thomas didn't send her packing over this, perhaps her mother would, simply so she could find some peace. The older woman had been conflict-averse, deferring always to her husband, then after his death, to her grown son.

Once breakfast was ready, they sat across from one another at the small kitchen table overlooking the cornfields.

"This is so *gut*." Inwardly Eve laughed at herself. How easily she had slipped into her native tongue. She had fought to lose the accent for fear a classmate might start asking questions about her background. As a journalist—as a private person—she never wanted to be the story. Fortunately, most people were only superficially interested in others and would allow her to turn the conversation back around to them.

They finished eating, then sat quietly over their coffee. "Your brother has made a nice life here."

Ah, my brother. Again.

A flicker of a smile touched her mother's lips. "Oh, and the twins keep Katy busy."

"I can imagine." Her childhood home had been abuzz with activity yesterday afternoon when she first arrived. "They are beautiful children." Growing up, she had been surrounded by large Amish families. The older children helped raise the younger ones, much like she had seen Mercy helping with her siblings.

Grandma Gerty opened her mouth, then paused, as if she was measuring her words. "Don't you want a family of your own?"

Eve jerked her head back, surprised at her mother's question. But then again, why should she be? Amish women were raised to be wives. Mothers. For her mother to have a twenty-five-year-old single daughter must feel strange.

Eve lifted a shoulder. She had been so busy carving out a life in the outside world, she had only made time for one man, and that had been a total disaster. She smiled ruefully. "I don't even have a boyfriend. So marriage isn't on my radar."

"Maybe you can meet someone while you're here." The hopeful tone in her mother's voice made Eve sad. She didn't want to be responsible for her mother's happiness, not in that way.

"Mother..." Eve made a big show of rolling her eyes, as if this were some big joke. Dylan's handsome face floated to mind, and she knew that wasn't what was being suggested. Any Amish parent would be encouraging their single daughters to marry within their faith.

"You know they'd forgive you." Her mother lifted her eyes to her youngest child. Something Eve couldn't quite identify flitted in their depths.

A ticking started in her head and a familiar outrage sparked in her belly. *Forgive me?* The anger wasn't directed at her mother so Eve blinked slowly and chose her words carefully. "I'm home for a visit, *Mem*. I want to make sure you're getting the best care. If you need it," she quickly added.

A deep line creased her mother's brow. "We've discussed this. I saw what my sister went through."

Eve reached across the table and touched her mother's hand, callused from a lifetime of honest work. "Please? All I ask is that you consider going to an appointment in Buffalo to see a respected oncologist." Eve couldn't leave things to chance.

You might not have a choice, a voice mocked her.

Her mother seemed to be studying their hands, then she looked up. "If I agree to this doctor"—her eyes flared wide, as if to emphasize *doctor*—"will you reconsider staying in Hunters Ridge?"

"Mem"—Eve hated the whine in her voice—"you know I can't do that."

A pale eyebrow arched and her mother waited her out. She had perfected the patient pause which was ultimately filled with guilty confessions or deep apologies.

Grandma Gerty had only asked her to reconsider. She hadn't asked for a commitment. "What does that look like to you, *Mem*?"

A smile flickered at the corners of her mother's lips and a light brightened her eyes. For the first time since Eve arrived yesterday, her mother seemed like her old self. "You'll live by the rules of the *Ordnung* while you're here."

A pinging started in Eve's brain as she considered what this meant. She didn't have to imagine long before her mother ticked off the items on her fingers.

"No car. No phone. Plain clothing."

Eve got twitchy at the mention of no phone. Like for most people, it had become a constant companion. Another appendage. "I'll need a car to get you to your appointment."

Her mother tipped her head and the long tie from her bonnet draped over her shoulder. "Fair enough. You can drive me there in *Englisch* clothes, if you prefer, but other than that, you follow the rules."

Eve rubbed her jaw slowly. It was a small price to pay.

She'd just be hanging around with her mother in her *dawdy haus* the rest of the time anyway. What could it hurt?

"Deal." Instinctively, Eve held out her hand, then dropped it. Mem wasn't the shaking hands type. "First I'd like to run into town to pick up a few things. It'll be easier with my car." And she wasn't quite ready to be seen out and about in plain clothing. She still needed her armor to face her past.

CHAPTER 8

A short time later, Eve ventured into town in her nondescript silver sedan that her brother had allowed her to park behind the barn. Her mother had also spoken to Thomas about Eve's visit and he begrudgingly agreed she could stay with their mother in the dawdy haus. However, it didn't come without an implied warning: *you cause trouble and you're out of here.* Eve accepted the offer, but as grateful as she wanted to be, she couldn't get past the notion that she had to seek his permission in the first place. It had been her childhood home. Her mother still lived there. Why did Thomas have all the control?

The years spent on her own had made her far too independent to start taking orders from her big brother. But she had to compromise. This was the price of helping Mem.

Eve shoved the thoughts aside and slowed and turned into the grocery store parking lot. Nothing had changed, not even the large sale signs in bold red letters covering the windows. She'd probably recognize the employees, too. Little evolved in a small town. She smiled at how easy it was to zip her car into a spot. As a teenager, she'd have to hitch her horse and buggy and tend to the animal. She supposed she'd gained some insight into why the Amish forbade vehicles: too simple to drive away from home and keep on going.

Eve aimed the key fob at her car and found herself glancing around, as if she was doing something wrong. Being back in Hunters Ridge made her itchy in her own skin. It was a very uncomfortable feeling. But she refused to allow Aaron Brenneman or her guilty conscience to chase her away. Not again.

Self-consciously, she dragged her fingers through her hair. Perhaps no one would recognize her now that she had blonde highlights and a shoulder-length cut. She also wore a touch of makeup, however it was far less than she wore when she was in front of the camera. Her camera makeup and her name change made her feel like a different person.

The reason for her trip into town had been twofold. First, she'd grab a few groceries for her and her mom, since Mem seemed to exist on coffee and cookies. At her brother's house, Eve noticed she had only moved food around the plate. The commotion of a large family with small children made it easy to miss her lack of appetite. Eve had to help her mother improve her nutrition.

Secondly, she had to call her friend Suze, back in Buffalo, to get the contact information for the oncologist she had once interviewed for a segment on *AM Morning*. She had thought she had the doctor's name in her phone, but she must have kept it in her desk on a business card. The cell reception was spotty at the farm. She wanted to have this conversation without yelling over static or repeating herself after realizing the connection had dropped.

As she approached the door of the grocery store, the pharmacy across the street caught her eye. Maybe the pharmacist could recommend an over-the-counter painkiller to help her mother. The local physician was a kindly elderly man who had no expertise in her mother's illness, but she needed to find a stopgap until she could get an appointment in Buffalo. It broke Eve's heart to watch her mother struggle with pain. She tried to hide it, but Eve noticed the subtle winces and quiet gasps.

After making her purchase with instructions on how to alternate the medications for best effect, Eve stepped back onto the sunny sidewalk. She still had to go to the grocery store, but she wasn't in a hurry. There was something depressing about being cooped up in the closed up *dawdy haus*. Her mother was constantly cold despite the summer heat.

Eve decided to take a stroll down Main Street and enjoy the warm sun. As she neared the diner, she stepped aside, allowing an Amish mother and her two children to pass in the other direction. The woman lowered her eyes and turned to make sure her two young children were following close behind. Eve's cheeks warmed as she realized she was the object of the woman's concern. The woman had passed too quickly for Eve to get a good look at her face, to know if she had been someone she used to hang out with. Hunters Ridge was a small town. And the Amish community within it, even smaller.

Eve remembered being that woman, so meek, so afraid of the outside world. She wished she could invite her for coffee and explain that she was no different than she was. They both had hopes and dreams. Loved their families, too. That *Englisch* people weren't evil. No more than Amish were evil. Bad people existed everywhere. So did good.

Eve lifted her hand and tucked a strand of hair behind her ear. She supposed it wasn't her mission to change everyone's opinion. She only needed to keep the peace with her family long enough to care for her mother.

"Eve," a tentative voice called to her.

"Yes?" Eve said automatically as she slowly turned around.

The Amish woman had returned, her head still slightly bowed, as if she had already changed her mind. Eve's attention was immediately drawn to her two small children who were now sitting quietly on a bench in front of the hardware store a short distance away.

Something in the hard set of the woman's eyes sparked recognition. "Lena? Lena Troyer?" The two women had grown up together but hadn't been especially close.

"It's Lena Brenneman now." The woman squared her shoulders, as if her words were a challenge.

Eve swallowed. "You're married to Aaron?"

"*Yah*. You need to leave him alone." Lena fidgeted with the trim of her blue cape that matched her long dress, making Eve feel underdressed in her shorts and T-shirt.

Eve forced a nervous smile and, in that moment, she decided to try another approach. "You have beautiful children."

"*Yah*, and you have to accept that he's married to me now."

Eve didn't need a mirror to imagine the look of shock on her face. "I have no idea what you're talking about." She tilted her head. "Did he tell you what happened last night?"

"He was out with his cousin and ran into you. He spared me the details, but it upset him so. I'm afraid he had too much to drink, and my husband doesn't usually drink. He's a *gut* man."

Everyone seemed to be saying that, but without action, Eve suspected they were hollow words. She bit back her anger.

Aaron was not a *gut* man and he was a liar. She met Lena's pleading gaze and decided unloading on her would be mean. Eve would leave Hunters Ridge after she got her mother settled, and Lena would still be stuck with good ol' Aaron.

"Rest assured, Lena, I have no interest in your husband. I am only in town because my mother is ill."

Lena's head jerked back, as if she had been bracing for an argument that never came. "Oh, I..." Her eyes immediately grew red-rimmed. Perhaps Eve had unwittingly proven her husband a liar. "I will keep her in my prayers."

Behind Lena, one of her children scooted off the bench and plucked a few petals from the marigolds in the pot in front of the store. "I think your daughter is picking a bouquet for you."

Lena's face colored and she spun around and grabbed her hand, scolding her. The Amish woman shot her a quick glance and Eve waved, then turned around. Whatever Lena had hoped to accomplish by confronting her, she had failed. However, it did make Eve wonder what kind of marriage they had. She suspected men like Aaron didn't change. She prayed he treated his wife and children well.

As a journalist, Eve always wondered about people. The stories behind the person. Maybe someday she'd be strong enough to return to Hunters Ridge and interview some of her former neighbors. Eve laughed to herself as she continued down Main Street. The biggest problem with that idea was that she was likely to become part of the story.

No, that isn't happening.

Eve found herself slowing down under the empty marquee. Nostalgia—longing—washed over her unexpectedly. Three red letters—R, C, D—hung at varying angles on the board, making her wonder what movie had last played at the now abandoned theater.

She drifted toward the entrance shadowed by the overhang. She lifted her hand to shield her eyes to get a better view inside the dark, empty theater. The same threadbare red carpet. The glass counter where she ordered Milk Duds and popcorn with extra butter from Dylan Kimble, the concession stand worker turned sheriff's deputy. And beyond that, the single auditorium where she'd take a seat near the back and wait—*hope*—Dylan would find her on his break and where they'd stay long after the movie and his break were over.

Eve wiped the dusty edge of her hand on her jean shorts. A hollow feeling expanded inside her. What would she say to teenage Eve? So naive, yet in the end so brave. She wondered if she'd have a chance to see Dylan again. It had been so unlikely that she had seen him at all, especially on her first night back to Hunters Ridge.

Why hadn't he followed through on his plans to become a lawyer?

Maybe he had met a local girl, fallen in love, and decided to stay put.

She could have been that girl.

In her dreams.

They were from two walks of life, and hers had imploded, forcing her to leave everyone she cared about behind.

Eve slid the tips of her fingers into her back pockets and studied the cracked sidewalk, trying hard to imagine her younger self crossing this same threshold. It was so strange to be back here. So, so strange…

Her buzzing phone snapped her out of her musings. She slid her hand into her open purse and grabbed it, checking the screen. Her good friend and coworker from the news station stuck her tongue out at her in the candid that Eve had selected for her contact photo. *Good.* Eve had been waiting for the call after sending her a text. She swiped the screen. "Hi, Suze."

"Hey there. How's it going?"

The two women had become friends first in college, then over the past few years working all hours at the news station. They had discussed the men they were dating and the restaurants they enjoyed and everything in between. Only after Eve had decided to return home to Hunters Ridge for an extended vacation had she finally confided in Suze about her Amish roots. Prior to then she had stuck to the simple story that she was estranged from her family. Because of that, Suze had welcomed her into her home. And Suze's mother, Carol Oliver, had become a second mother of sorts, or perhaps the proper word was mentor.

"Quiet out here." *Mostly*. Eve decided not to share the visit from her drunk ex last night because she knew Suze would pepper her with questions she didn't care to answer.

"Must be a relief not to have to look over your shoulder now that you're out of Buffalo."

Eve laughed, but it came off as strangled. "What did your mother say—'You haven't made it until you have a few overzealous fans.'"

"She would know." Anytime Suze's mother came up in conversation, Suze's tone turned sarcastic. The mother-daughter relationship seemed strained, perhaps because they were both working in the same industry, and Suze seemed to tire of the comparisons when people heard her last name. "I swear she thought it was a badge of honor. I could tell you stories."

"Please don't. I have enough stress right now."

"Don't worry. Things seem to have calmed down here. It's probably good you took a little vacation. Whoever's been harassing you will move on to his next target."

"From your lips to God's ears."

"Whatever..." Suze laughed, an infectious sound that drew people to her. "Do like Carol and don't sweat it."

Suze's mother continued to wield her influence by tapping into endless paid speaking gigs. If someone was anyone in Buffalo, Carol Oliver knew them, and they most likely owed her a favor. Eve had been in awe. Suze, of course, was unimpressed by her mother. Yet Carol—it always struck Eve as disrespectful that Suze called her mother by her first name—had found in Eve an enthusiastic student, even if Eve's goals had never been to be on camera.

"How's *your* mom?" Suze asked, changing the subject.

"I don't know. She's aged so much since I've been gone."

"I'm sorry. That's tough. Has she been to any doctor yet?" Her voice moved up in pitch. "The Amish aren't one of those groups that don't believe in medicine, are they?"

"No, no, it's a personal decision." Part of the reason Eve never told people she had grown up Amish was because she didn't want to answer all the probing questions. They were honest, well-meaning questions for the most part but Eve feared, in Suze's case, she might try to press her to do a story on what it was like growing up Amish, something Eve would never agree to do. Eve was already out of her comfort zone on camera. She had thought her career in journalism would be in print. Or at least behind the scenes. And here she was, climbing the ladder in front of the camera. "You've seen Amish people at Buffalo General Hospital, haven't you?" Eve asked.

More than once Eve had been called down to the hospital to cover a story and came up short when she saw an Amish family in their plain clothing taking over the lobby as they worried about their hospitalized loved one. Each time, Eve studied their faces, wondering if she'd see someone from Hunters Ridge. She never had.

"Yeah, you're right. I guess their way of life boggles my mind."

"Hey," Eve said, eager to get back to the reason she had

wanted to talk to Suze in the first place, "did you get the number for Dr. Isabella Moretti?"

"Did one better," Suze said. "I know you were having cell phone reception problems out in the sticks."

"Oh yeah?" Eve turned toward the theater doors to hide her face from the construction workers walking toward her on the sidewalk. She put one hand over her ear to drown out their lunch-break chatter.

"I got her an appointment."

"Oh...great...thanks." Eve was often amazed by Suze's boldness. She took charge when Eve had a tendency to hold back. Yet they made a great team at work. Suze's "go get 'em" spirit and Eve's attention to detail. They complemented one another's style. Eve was going to miss working with her day in and day out now that Eve was moving to the morning show as on-air talent. Butterflies fluttered in her belly at the thought. On camera, every day.

"How's..." Suze hesitated, as if she was checking something. "Wednesday at two? I'll text you the information."

"That's great. Really great. Thank you."

"You're welcome. Hey, do you have another sec? I've got to tell you the funniest story." Eve started walking back toward her car. "We had to be in downtown Buffalo for some fluff piece about an event at Canalside. Some brewpub wanted me to taste their newest flavor and it was yuck." Eve could imagine her friend twisting up her face. "I didn't spit it out, but I near choked. Then I got the giggles on camera." Suze laughed in the retelling, then she seemed to sober. "I'm never going to make it in this profession if I can't stay composed." She sighed heavily. "You are always so much better than me at that."

Eve considered her words carefully. She didn't want to be condescending, but she was happy to consider someone else's problems other than her own. She had remembered the hollow words of consolation when a man she had thought she loved stepped right over her to get a key internship she had also been in line for. "You're a great journalist. Smart. Thorough. And we both know the viewers love when reporters lose it a little bit, especially on those fluff pieces. And you are always better at getting the interviews we need. You never take no for an answer."

"Yeah..." Her friend's bubbly laughter sounded across the line. "I'll never forget the taste of that raunchy beer."

Eve looked both ways and crossed the street to the grocery store parking lot.

"Listen to me going on," Suze said. "You probably have to go."

"I've enjoyed catching up. And thanks again for snagging that appointment. I appreciate it." The paper pharmacy bag crumpled as she dug through her purse to find the key fob.

"Of course. What are best friends for?"

Eve opened her car door, tossed the meds onto the passenger seat, and locked it up and started walking toward the store, listening to Suze start another story, something she often did even as she suggested ending the call. A car pulled up and the driver got out and called to her.

"Hold on, Suze." Eve lowered the phone. Then to the stranger, she said, "Yes?"

"You've got a flat."

Eve walked around the car. Her front passenger tire was indeed flat. Eve bent over and ran her hand over the rubber and found the head of a wide nail sticking out of the wall. "Just great," she muttered. She lifted the phone to her ear. "I've got a flat." Her heartbeat raced in her ears. "Looks like I picked up something from the road."

"Did you drive through a construction site?"

"Not that I'm aware of."

"Could it have been intentional?" Suze asked innocently enough.

"I wonder," Eve whispered, more to herself than to Suze. Familiar icy dread pooled in her belly.

"I'm so sorry, sweetie," Suze said. "Seems you have bad luck wherever you go."

CHAPTER 9

"Hey Mason, buddy, you have to stay next to me." Dylan held out his hand to his nephew who insisted on touching each and every paintbrush in his line of sight. Dylan had taken the day off to pick up the paint and supplies to work on his four-year-old nephew's bedroom. He pulled out a small brush and handed it to the boy. "This looks about your size."

Mason took the brush and a huge smile split his adorable little face. The same smile as Dylan's twin brother. A bittersweet reminder that never failed to ping Dylan's heart with all the could-have-beens and if-onlys. "Can we paint dinosaurs on my wall, too?"

Dylan touched his blond mop of hair. All the old photos of Dylan and Jacob showed the two boys with fair hair before it turned darker in their adolescence. "I'm not sure I know how to paint dinosaurs, but maybe we can find some sort of stickers or something for the wall." He looked up and scanned the signs over the aisles in the hardware store. "If they don't have anything here, we can take a road trip to one of the bigger stores."

"Can I go, too?" Mason loved to tag along with his uncle.

"Of course, little man. Now let's pick out a color. What are you thinking?" Dylan took Mason's free hand and led him to the paint samples on small cards.

His nephew's eyes scanned all the colors. He scrunched up his determined face and reached up and grabbed a rectangular swatch of four shades of orange. "I like these!"

Dylan tilted his head, considering. His mother Tessa had told Mason he could pick any color he wanted, but orange? Dylan was careful to school his expression and wondered if he should steer his nephew toward more neutral greens or blues, like his mother had done while discouraging him from putting socks on with his sandals.

Dylan took the swatch from Mason and studied it. Before he had a chance to ask him which orange on the sample card, his phone buzzed in his back pocket. *Good.* Maybe he could run this decision by his mother before he bought a gallon of orange paint.

Dylan looked at the screen and didn't recognize the number. He might have ignored it but something compelled him to answer it. "Hello."

"Dylan?" The single word was all it took. He was twenty-one again and sitting in the back of the theater. He reached down absentmindedly and touched Mason's head to make sure he stayed close.

"Yes?" A long sigh came over the line. "What's going on, Eve?"

She laughed, but she didn't sound like she was having a good day. "How'd you know it was me?"

He smiled and stared blindly toward Main Street. "Familiar voice." He quickly changed the subject. "Is something wrong?"

"I'm sorry to call you, but I didn't know who else…" She let her words trail off before continuing. "I don't exactly have a lot of friends in Hunters Ridge. Anyway..." She seemed to sense she was rambling. "I came into town to run some errands and now I have a flat tire. I tried to change it myself, but the thingy won't budge."

"The thingy, huh?" Next to him, Mason used his paintbrush to pretend paint the color-swatch display case using dramatic up and down arm motions. "Where are you?"

"In the grocery store parking lot on Main Street." Her voice sounded far away, then grew closer. "Could you recommend a garage? Maybe someone could come out and help me?"

"Not too many options in Hunters Ridge." He pulled the phone away from his mouth and whispered to his nephew, "Come on, buddy." They walked toward the cash register to pay for the paintbrush.

"True." He could imagine her scrunching up her cute nose like she did when she wasn't happy with how a movie ended. "I guess I could do a Google search and see what pops up."

"No need, I'm on Main Street. I'll be there in a heartbeat."

"No, no, I didn't mean—" Eve stopped talking abruptly, perhaps reconsidering his offer. "If you don't think it would be too much trouble."

"Of course not. Hang tight." Dylan ended the call, paid for the paintbrush and headed out onto the street and squinted into the bright sunlight.

"We didn't get the paint, Uncle Dylan," Mason said, twisting around awkwardly toward the hardware store while clutching his uncle's hand.

"We'll get the paint later. I have to help a friend first."

Dylan aimed the key fob at his truck and it chirped as he unlocked the door. The grocery store was close, but he wanted to move the truck so he could change her tire.

Mason hopped up into the back seat, and Dylan buckled

him into his car seat. He tapped his nephew gently on his knee. "Ready, buddy?"

Mason's eyebrows squished together. "You have a friend?"

Dylan laughed. *Out of the mouths of babes.* He believed his nephew came by it honestly. The little boy had only viewed Dylan in his capacity as an uncle, surrounded by family. "I do have a friend."

Or at least he did, once upon a time.

When Dylan and Mason arrived at the grocery store, he found Eve leaning on the side of her car, her head dipped while she scrolled on her phone. The sunlight hit on her blonde highlights making her hair much lighter than he had remembered. She had on jean shorts and a T-shirt with a slogan he couldn't make out, and he wasn't about to stare. If he hadn't been called out to her family farm last night, he probably would have walked right past her. Oh, he would have noticed her, but he wouldn't have recognized her as the young Amish girl he'd befriended at his part-time job.

When he pulled up with the driver's side window down, she looked up at him blankly at first, then a slow smile brightened her face. Her response did something to his insides that he was afraid to explore.

"I was searching online for a garage," she said, then lowered her phone.

"Let me take a look."

"Sure thing." She pushed off the car and walked toward the flat.

Dylan parked behind her vehicle. "I'll be a sec, okay?" he said over his shoulder. He left the truck running with the AC on, but left the front window open so he could hear his nephew.

He climbed out and walked over to the vehicle. He ran his hand along the outside wall of the tire. "Looks like you got a nail."

"I saw that."

"It's in an odd location." He straightened and glanced around the lot, confirming what he already knew. "No sense looking for cameras. There aren't any in this lot. The sheriff's department knows all their locations. Some places insist on not having them, out of respect for the Amish."

"Wait. This wasn't an accident?" Her pretty brown eyes widened and her mouth flattened.

He held up his hand and stopped short of touching her arm. "I didn't say that. It does seem at an odd spot, though. It would be up in the threads if you picked it up on the road."

"How did this happen?" She dragged a hand through her silky hair and he had to force himself to look away. The Eve he knew always had her hair twisted into a bun and tucked under a bonnet.

"There's no telling. Could have been there for a little while, producing a slow leak."

"So maybe I picked it up in Buffalo, either accidentally or someone did it on purpose?" She bit her pink lip. "But maybe it happened here in town?" Something akin to annoyance flashed in the depths of her eyes. He had seen that look last night.

"Aaron Brenneman was out at your family's place harassing you. Do you have reason to believe he'd do this?"

Eve's gaze snapped up to his and she muttered something quietly that sounded like, "That was over seven years ago."

"What's the history with Aaron?"

Eve stared at him for a long moment, then blinked and dragged her fingers through her hair. "That's ancient history." Her tone lacked conviction.

"I can go over to his place and talk to him." He glanced back at his truck. Mason was hidden behind tinted rear windows. He could run his nephew home, then shoot over to the Brenneman farm.

Eve frowned. "That's not a good idea."

"You're going to have to give me more here, Eve." He fought to keep the frustration out of his voice.

"I'm at the mercy of my brother. If I cause problems, he'll ask me to leave."

Dylan suddenly realized he'd do anything to remove the worry from her eyes. Back in their theater days he had loved making her laugh. "Eve, if this Brenneman guy is harassing you, we have to put a stop to it."

"He was drunk." She lifted a shoulder, seemingly trying to dismiss his behavior. "You said yourself that I could have picked up this nail a while ago. Maybe in Buffalo or somewhere between there and here." She crossed her arms. "I need to keep things low-key so I can take care of my mom."

"Are you sure?" She had a point. They had no evidence someone tampered with her tire even though the placement of the nail was odd.

"Let's go..." Mason called from the back seat through the open driver's side window.

Eve's eyes widened, obviously surprised that he had a passenger. Dylan smiled and said to her, "Hold up a second." He walked a few feet over to look into the back seat at Mason. "Okay, buddy. I'm almost done here."

Dylan turned to Eve and she held up her phone, an apologetic expression on her face. "Don't let me hold you up. Tell me the name of a trustworthy garage and I'll call them."

Dylan shook his head and walked over to the flat. He leaned over and picked up the lug wrench she had abandoned on the pavement. "Did you check that you had a spare?"

She playfully rolled her eyes at him. "One comes with the car, right?"

"Yes, one comes with the car." He felt a smile pulling at his lips. "I'll change the tire. It won't take long."

Eve's cheeks heated as she watched Dylan work the lug wrench, his tan biceps bulging under the short sleeves of his blue T-shirt. Blue was a good color on him. She briefly closed her eyes and turned away, afraid she'd get caught staring.

Uh, this man has a son. Who's sitting in the car. And most likely a wife somewhere.

Eve drifted over to the truck. Dylan had introduced her to "my buddy, Mason" when he cut off the engine and opened all the windows before grabbing the spare and getting to work. Eve leaned on the window frame. The child was busy painting every surface with a dry paintbrush. "Are you getting ready to do some painting?"

"Yes! We're going to paint my bedroom orange!" The child ended each comment with an exclamation point. Eve laughed.

The boy smiled and she was struck by how much he looked like his father. He had the same brown eyes and dimple on his chin. Yep, definitely his son. The realization was bittersweet, yet if her mother hadn't gotten sick and if Aaron hadn't come to her house in a drunken stupor, Eve wouldn't have even seen Dylan Kimble during her return visit. So why did she feel like her future was being sucked away from her?

She dismissed her spiraling thoughts as nostalgia for a simpler time. She swallowed and found her voice. "Orange is a bold choice. Why did you pick that color?"

"It's sunny."

"It is. I'm sure it will be great."

"We forgot to buy the paint," the boy said, his prior enthusiasm shifting quickly to dramatic disappointment in the slump of his shoulders. He lifted his paintbrush and stretched against the constraints of his car seat to drag the bristles across the roof of the truck.

"Maybe you can pick it up when you're done here." Eve had a mental image of the father and son spreading out tarps in the little boy's bedroom. Dylan was probably a very patient dad. Maybe his wife would help. Eve found herself wondering what kind of woman he had married. Someone he had met at college? Someone local?

"Can you unlock the back door?" Dylan asked. "I want to move some things from the trunk to make room for the flat." His deep voice vibrated through her.

"Thanks." She grabbed the key fob from the back pocket of her jeans. "Here." Dylan took it from her, his fingers brushing against the palm of her hand. An unexpected shiver raced up her arm.

Heaven help me. It had been a long time since she had dated anyone, and she had sworn off dating because she hadn't had much luck. Dylan was just a friendly, familiar face during a turbulent time. Besides, he was married.

Eve focused on making small talk with the kid while Dylan finished up with the tire.

When he was done, he approached, rubbing his hands together. "You're all set."

"I can't thank you enough," Eve said.

"I'm hungry!" the child announced from the back seat. "I want french fries."

"Mason, you're being rude." Dylan lifted an eyebrow that was meant to be a reprimand, but the quirk of his lips seemed to undermine his authority. "But a man's gotta eat when a man's gotta eat, right?" His hand hovered over the small of Eve's back, radiating warmth and a feeling that she had no right to explore.

"Can I pay you?" she asked, suddenly feeling foolish. "Your time..."

Dylan's forehead crumbled and a flash of disappointment sparked in his eyes. "Don't be silly. It was my pleasure. I'm glad you called."

"Yeah." *He's married.* "I don't know anyone here, except the Amish, and well…" *Stop rambling.* "They don't exactly have cars and I promised my mother I'd try to follow the rules." She inwardly cringed at the giggle that slipped out.

"Want to join us for lunch?" Dylan asked.

Butterflies flitted in her stomach. "I shouldn't."

Dylan lifted an eyebrow. "Not hungry?"

"I just…" It seemed silly to say it didn't seem appropriate because he had a wife and family, because that meant she considered the invitation to be more than it was: a simple lunch invitation. For someone so mature, she certainly stunk at this whole boy-girl interaction thing, especially when it came to her first crush.

Unrequited first love.

"Come on, Uncle Dylan. I'm hungry!" Mason yelled from the back seat.

Uncle Dylan. Her heart kick-started and a warm flush of excitement washed over her.

"Oh, this is your nephew?" Relief raced through her. How pathetic was she? "I thought…he looks—" She dropped off midsentence.

"Mason is my twin brother's son."

Of course. Does this mean he's single? Hope bubbled up inside her. Inwardly she shook her head. Why did it matter? She'd be returning to Buffalo soon.

"Come on, grab something to eat with us. I can swing you back to pick up your car after we're done."

"Okay." She valued his friendship at least. What could lunch hurt? Especially with the little guy—his *nephew!*—as their chaperone.

They both hopped into the cab of his truck. Dylan shifted

in his seat. "I hope you don't mind burgers and fries. There's a great place not too far."

"Sure." Eve reached behind her and tugged on the seat belt and secured it with a solid click. "I appreciate your help."

"Did you need to let your mom know you'll be running late?"

"I see you're still thoughtful."

"I try." He pressed the ignition button, put the truck into gear and they pulled out onto Main Street.

"My mom's not expecting me for a while." Eve had mentioned taking care of some business in town and that she'd be home before dinner. "So, Mason's your nephew. How is your brother?" They had covered a lot of ground talking about their respective backgrounds in the back of the theater. Dylan had been fascinated by her large family. She had been equally intrigued by his small one. She wondered what it would be like to have a twin. They joked that the *Englisch* didn't have as many children because they didn't need the manpower like the Amish did to run their farms.

Dylan sucked in his lips, shot a concerned glance in the rearview mirror at the little boy, then at her. Had she said something wrong?

"My daddy's in heaven," Mason announced as simply and non-dramatically as if he had announced his dad was at work or at home cutting the lawn.

Her face flushed hot and unease pooled in her belly. Dylan had been close to his twin brother. She bit back an apology, not sure how to navigate this conversation with their audience of one in the back seat.

"Mason and I have plans to paint his bedroom." Dylan graciously bailed her out after she had inserted foot in mouth. "We were at the hardware store when you called."

"We didn't get the paint I wanted," Mason said, not for the first time. Eve shifted her head to watch the little boy run the bristles of the brush over the seat next to him. He then waved it around as if it was a magic wand. "I have my own brush and I get to help. We're going to put dinosaurs on the wall, too."

"I like to paint, but I'm not a big fan of the prep work, or the cleanup," Eve said absentmindedly. She recalled the pride of moving into her first apartment and fixing it up exactly how she wanted. The Amish weren't much into decorating and even the simplest artwork gave her great joy.

"Benji can't help," Mason announced, seeming eager to give her the rundown.

"Benji's his six-year-old brother," Dylan explained. Then to Mason: "Remember how we painted Benji's room last summer? Now it's your turn."

"My belly is rumbling," Mason said, taking the conversation back to food.

"We're almost there." Dylan glanced over at Eve. "I hope you're hungry, too."

CHAPTER 10

"Thanks for coming with me to drop Mason off. I hadn't realized how late it had gotten." Dylan put the truck into drive. He waved to his nephews Mason and Benji standing on the porch with Tessa. Mason happily waved back with his paintbrush in hand. The bristles bent every which way, but Dylan didn't care. A few bucks for hours of fun, and he'd pick up a small trim roller for his nephew before they actually started painting. "If he didn't have soccer this afternoon, the little guy would have convinced me to start working on his room today."

"They're lucky to have you in their lives," Eve said as she watched his brother's family from the passenger window. He stole a glance at her pretty long hair pooling around her shoulders before she turned and seemed surprised that he was staring. "I'm sorry about your brother."

"Thanks." It had been a while since someone had expressed their condolences. Living, working, growing up in a small town, everyone knew your business. Had already regarded him with pity in their eyes, when they couldn't find the words. People were funny about death. Certainly not in a humorous way, but in an oddly curious one. They could talk to you six ways to Sunday about the weather, sports, nonsense. But death—especially when it came suddenly, tragically, and to the young—was another story.

Eve didn't follow up with a question about the circumstances of his brother's death, but he felt compelled to tell her. Maybe sitting this close to her in the confines of his truck was reminiscent of their back-of-the-theater days. Their relationship had started out in the most random of ways. When the movie ended, he had to sweep up dropped popcorn and litter, and she offered to hold the dustpan. Then he asked her if she liked the movie. The conversations grew from there into a friendship that didn't extend beyond the dark theater. He had seen her once in town when she was with her family, but she dipped her head and turned her face away. He had taken the hint. But she kept returning and they continued to talk about everything under the sun. And now she was here, seated next to him, dressed in regular clothes and as pretty as he remembered. *Prettier.*

He scrubbed a hand across his face. "Jacob died of an overdose." The words felt hollow. The raw emotion had been wrung out of him in the three years since Tessa had called him in a panic. *He won't wake up! He won't wake up!*

"I'm…I…I didn't mean to pry." Eve pressed her palms together and squeezed them between her knees, seeming to draw into herself.

"You're not prying. Everyone around here knows. I suppose we're the cautionary tale. One brother goes into law enforcement, the other doesn't wake up one morning after too much alcohol and prescription drugs."

"That's awful. I'm so, so sorry."

He always felt the need to explain one last thing. "He broke his back when we were teenagers. He fell out of a tree stand while we were hunting. Doctors gave him something for pain." He left it at that. Anyone who followed the news could fill in the rest of the story.

Dylan and his brother would laugh and talk smack for hours on end out in the woods. Their trips never resulted in a kill. They did it because most of their friends were big hunters. Everyone skipped school the first day of hunting season. It was a rite of passage. It wasn't supposed to change the course of their lives.

Dylan stared straight ahead at the road, forcing himself to not feel anything, not anymore. It was such a darn shame that if he let his emotions in, he wasn't sure he'd recover. Instead, he focused his energy on sticking around Hunters Ridge to be the father figure for his nephews.

As if reading his mind, she said, "Mason and Benji are lucky to have you."

"They'd be luckier if they still had their dad." He clenched the steering wheel.

Eve bit her lower lip before asking, "Do you have children of your own?"

"Nope." He tipped his head from side to side, trying to ease the knots that tightened every time he thought of his brother's senseless death. "How about you?" He found himself stealing glances at her beautiful face, waiting for the answer.

"No children."

His gaze drifted down to her hand in her lap, then back to the road. He had noticed before that she didn't have on a ring. That didn't mean there wasn't a boyfriend back home. He couldn't imagine someone like her being single, but he wasn't going to come out and ask. She had already mentioned that she wasn't going to be in Hunters Ridge for long.

They drove in silence until they reached the center of town. He pulled into the grocery store parking lot. The smaller donut tire appeared out of place on her car. "Here you go."

"Thanks again." She seemed hesitant to get out of the truck, and if he was being honest, he hated to see her go. "It was nice catching up, meeting your nephews." She looked like she had something else on her mind. "I'm sorry about your brother." She narrowed her gaze. "How has the rest of your life been? You talked about becoming a lawyer."

Dylan tugged on his seat belt, as if it might ease the strain on his chest. "My brother's death changed a lot of things." He shook his head. "I know that sounds awful, but…" He closed his eyes and gritted his jaw. When he opened them again, an Amish couple was crossing in front of his truck. The man held a sack of groceries. Their horse and buggy were hitched to a post in the far corner of the lot. "I had joined the sheriff's department to save some money before applying to law school. I couldn't afford to go right after getting my undergrad. Then my brother died and it made more sense to stay close to home. That's the short story." Dylan shifted in his seat, the familiar unease twisting his gut. "What have you been up to?" He needed to change the subject. And that seemed like a pretty good catch-all question without sounding too needy like, *Why didn't you say goodbye before leaving?* Or, *Are you in a relationship?*

"Well, I recently got a promotion at work."

"Oh yeah?" He realized he had no idea what she had been up to for seven years. "Tell me about it."

"I've been working at a local news station in Buffalo, mostly behind the scenes. However, lately I've gotten more airtime and"—she held up her palms—"you're looking at the new on-air talent for the *AM Morning* show in Buffalo. I don't suppose you've seen it?" She watched him expectantly.

Dylan shook his head. "Don't have a TV." This was the first time he honestly regretted not owning one.

"You and the rest of Hunters Ridge." She laughed. "Who would have thought a little Amish girl would grow up to have a career in television?"

"You used to write," he said, remembering how she talked about her journals.

She shifted in her seat. "You remember that?"

He wanted to say that he remembered everything about her, but he kept his wits about him. "Sure, why not? We discussed a lot while we ate those huge tubs of popcorn. And Milk Duds."

Eve winced. "I still can't eat buttered popcorn to this day. I overdid it back then."

He laughed. "Can't say I'm a fan either. You know"—he jerked his chin in the general direction of the old theater—"it's closed down now. Kids have to go to Fredonia if they want to catch a movie."

"I think most people stream movies at home. You don't have to listen to people chatting in the back of the theater." A light gleamed in her eyes. "Unless they don't have a TV, like you."

"You know what it's like to not have a TV."

She scoffed, clearly enjoying herself. "I was Amish. I didn't have a choice. Anyway, I'll be on *AM Morning* bright and early Monday through Friday starting right after Labor Day."

"Ah, so you have a few weeks to sleep in."

"No one sleeps in on a farm. Well, I do have the next two weeks off, and I have a little wiggle room to take off a couple more if necessary." She gently ran a finger under her eye. "I need to arrange for my mother's care." She pulled her phone out of her purse and glanced at the screen then dropped it back in, as if that might provide some answers.

"If there's anything I can do?" He raised his eyebrows.

Eve smiled tightly. "This lunch was a nice distraction. Thank you."

"Any time." He shifted and drummed his thumbs on the steering wheel. "Any chance we could do this again?"

For reasons he didn't understand, her cheeks fired pink. "Um, I want to spend as much time as I can with my mom. And I also promised her I'd play by the rules."

"Play by the rules?"

"Yeah, Amish rules." She flicked her fingers up and down her casual summer wardrobe. "After today, I will magically transfrom back to Plain Eve."

He tilted his head and studied her. "I remember Plain Eve. She wasn't half bad."

"Ha!" she said and reached for the passenger door handle. "Since I agreed to play by the rules, my mother agreed to a consult in Buffalo." She quickly pointed at him with bright eyes. "But for that, I negotiated wearing my regular clothes."

"Sounds like your mom drives a hard bargain."

"No way I'm going to have someone recognize me and snap my photo. I'd never live that down. I have a professional reputation to maintain." She closed her eyes briefly and shook her head. "Don't get me wrong. I'm not ashamed I grew up Amish. I just don't want that to be part of my bio." She shrugged. "Maybe that makes me sound shallow. I don't know."

"You don't have to explain anything to me."

She slid out of the truck then turned to face him through the open door. "I know." She paused for a heartbeat. "It was great to see you, Dylan."

"Great to see you, too." He felt the moment slipping away and he wanted to grab hold of it. "I just might have to buy a TV, since that's the only way I'm going to get to see you again."

A slow smile spread across her face and lit her eyes. "I'll be on super early in the morning."

He mirrored her smile. "Good thing I have an alarm clock."

Eve laughed, stepped back, and slammed the door shut. He watched her cross in front of his truck and then remembered her tire. He pressed the button to lower his window. "You don't want to be driving around on that little donut tire for long."

"Oh…" Eve's gaze drifted to her car, as if she hadn't thought about that. "Yeah, you're right."

"I'll pick up a new tire and come by your place tomorrow." When she twisted her pretty pink lips in indecision, he added, "Really, it's no bother."

"That would be great because I have to drive into Buffalo on Wednesday with my mother. You have my number?" She aimed her key fob and a double chirp sounded from her car.

"It came up on my caller ID." Dylan smiled. Another excuse to see her. "See you tomorrow." He suddenly felt better about saying goodbye. "And one more thing. Deputy Caitlin Flagler"—he tilted his head—"from last night. She didn't find either of the Brennemans walking on the road, or a vehicle. She drove out to his house and kept going. Everything looked quiet at their place."

Something akin to relief flashed across her face. "Thanks for letting me know." She waved in dismissal. "I'd prefer to let that situation die down, so I'm glad the deputy didn't knock on his door."

"Promise me you'll call me immediately if he comes looking for you." Eve was being evasive, but Dylan had a strong hunch something major had happened between the Brenneman guy and Eve. Maybe she'd eventually trust him enough to confide in him again.

She nodded slowly. Silent agreement, or simply a way to

change the subject? "Thanks again." She turned on her heel and pulled open her car door.

After watching Eve get in her car and drive away, he got on the road. His brother's memory weighed heavily on his mind. Jacob was never far from his thoughts, but even more so when he shared the story of his addiction and death. There were so many unanswered questions and what-ifs when it came to his brother.

And as he neared home, his thoughts cycled around to another great regret of his life—that his friendship with Eve Reist had ended abruptly without so much as a goodbye. He'd never get a second chance with his brother, but maybe, just maybe, he'd get a second chance with her.

CHAPTER 11

Eve hadn't even arrived home and she was already worried about how it would look when Dylan Kimble showed up tomorrow to replace her tire. She rolled her eyes at herself. Amazing how being back here made her feel like the awkward, shy Amish girl who had little say over her own life.

She had heard the rumors swirl around her when she was a teenager. Dylan was just one small piece. *She meets an* Englisch *boy in the back of the theater all the time!* That helpful tidbit from Aaron's younger sister. Eve wouldn't have been the first young Amish woman to have a romance—not that what she and Dylan had was a romance—with a townie, but that rumor, coupled with what happened with Aaron, made her realize she could never stay in Hunters Ridge. Her reputation had been damaged beyond repair. Even worse, no one chose to do anything about the person who had ruined it. It was her word against his.

When she reached the farm, her heart dropped when she saw a horse and buggy in the lane. *Visitors.* She wondered if she could sneak into her mother's house without being seen, but her car was like a neon sign blazing a trail up the lane to her parking spot behind the barn. When she climbed out, she realized that she had completely forgotten to stop at the grocery store. Well, at least she had some pain meds for her mother. And an appointment in Buffalo with the oncologist on Wednesday afternoon.

With a sense of purpose and her head angled down, she strode directly toward the *dawdy haus*, willing herself to be invisible. Something that shouldn't be so hard. With her hand on the doorknob, she heard her brother call out to her from across the way. She grumbled her frustration and slowly turned around, arranging a pleasant expression on her face. Thomas stood on his porch with the door to the house open behind him.

"Eve, there's a visitor here for you."

Her mouth went dry. "Let me drop this off to Mem. I'll be right over."

"Mother is here."

"Um, okay." Eve tossed the pharmacy bag and her purse on the rocking chair outside her mother's door, then crossed the yard, tugging down on the hem of her jean shorts, feeling exposed. She was not in the mood for visitors, especially ones who arrived in a buggy.

Thomas gave her a disgusted once-over as she passed by on her way into her childhood home. Her heart plummeted. The bishop sat on the bench along the back wall, and Eve crossed her arms in front of her, a protective gesture.

"Guder nammidaag." Good afternoon. "I wasn't expecting visitors," Eve muttered.

"I suspect not," the bishop said. His stern expression wasn't unfamiliar to Eve.

"How are you doing, Grandma Gerty?" Eve shifted her focus.

"Gut," Her mother sat in a rocker next to the cold wood-

burning stove. The skin under her eyes seemed darker today, or perhaps Eve was ultrasensitive to any signs of illness.

"Your brother mentioned you were home." The bishop ran his hand down his gray, wiry beard that hung to the middle of his chest. "Your mother led me to believe you'd be following the rules of the *Ordnung* while you were here."

Despite Eve's efforts to not overreact to his rebuke, her cheeks grew fiery hot. "As you're aware, my mother has been sick. I had to go into town to pick up some medication for her."

"I have been doing a perfectly *gut* job of taking care of Mem," her brother said defensively.

"I am grateful for that." Eve looked past him toward the kitchen, wondering where the rest of the family was. She imagined Katy forcing them to all sit quietly upstairs in their bedrooms so they wouldn't have to witness the confrontation.

The familiar combination of shame and anger twisted in her gut. She was a good person even if she didn't follow the Amish way, yet they'd never understand or accept her unless she returned fully in the eyes of the church.

She smiled tightly at her mother. "I believe we need to explore options for your care. There have been amazing advancements since Aunt Marian was sick." She decided to preempt their argument. "We have to see what we're dealing with."

"Your brother assures me that Gerty is content as things are," the bishop said.

Eve's gaze drifted to her brother, then to the bishop, her pulse beating wildly in her ears. "Ignoring the situation isn't an option." The bishop's head jerked back at her snappy reply, but that didn't deter her. "I've been able to get an appointment with a top oncologist in Buffalo." She walked over to her mother and placed her hand on her shoulder.

She's so thin. A shock raced through her and she had to steady her voice. "Isn't that great?"

"I'm not sure," she said softly, obviously conflicted, unsure who to please.

Please yourself for once, Mem! "I thought we already discussed this. That you'd go for a consult." Disappointment pulsed through her.

She stepped away from her mother and crossed her arms. She had to mount a defense against her brother—and now the bishop—and she truly wished she had put on the plain dress that her mother had laid out for her this morning. At the time it seemed silly. Like, why wear Amish clothing if she was going to drive her car into town? But her casual shorts and T-shirt weakened her argument that her presence was for the best. It also served as a reminder to the bishop that she was the girl who'd once made strong accusations against his grandson.

When they didn't respond, she added, "Thomas, you agreed, too."

"We should let mother decide." Thomas's gaze drifted to their mother whose ambivalence was written all over her narrow face.

"I don't like to go far from home," her mother whispered.

Anger ticked in Eve's brain as she fought the sinking feeling in her gut. "You can't give up." Gritting her teeth, she turned to the church leader. "I'm sorry, Bishop Leroy, but my mother's care shouldn't be any of your concern. I will do my best to respect the rules while I'm home, but I am taking her to Buffalo on Wednesday."

The bishop lifted his head, the regal way those in authority did when they didn't need to say anything to get their message across. There was a silent threat there, but she had been away for far too long to pinpoint its specificity.

"Eve, leave it alone," Thomas said.

She studied her brother's face, then the bishop's, realization dawning. "This doesn't have to do with Mother's treatment. It has to do with your grandson's drunken visit here last night."

The bishop had the common decency to flinch. He reached out and placed his wrinkled hands one on top of the other on the cane planted in front of him. "Aaron is married with two children. You are not going to cause him trouble."

Eve gritted her teeth. She felt like a teenager again. *Good ol' Aaron.* "Perhaps he should have stayed home with his family instead of trying to get into my window after a night of drinking."

"Eve!" Thomas scolded her. "Whoever keeps his mouth and his tongue keeps himself out of trouble." Was her brother reciting Bible verses for her benefit or the bishop's? "You know better than to gossip," he added more plainly while shooting nervous glances at the bishop.

"It's not gossip when it's the truth." Eve took a step backward, suddenly feeling hot and nauseous in the closed-up confines of her brother's house. She had a flashback to another time when the bishop came to this very house to get a confession out of her, but she had refused. "If you'll excuse me, I have to go." She hated the tremble in her voice.

"Wait," Thomas called out. "Do not walk away from us. You're being disrespectful."

Eve bit back her retort, knowing it wouldn't do anything to help her case. She needed his permission to remain with her mother. She didn't like it, but that was how things were. She stared at them, waiting for either of them to say what they really wanted to say.

"You are under the *Bann* until you return on bended knee," the bishop said. "Your mother would be wise to remember that."

Rage thrummed in her ears. "My mother needs me. She

hasn't done anything wrong." According to the rules of the *Ordnung*, her mem should be shunning her. Guilting her into returning to the Amish. Not making it easy for her to come and go. Eve rubbed her sweaty hands together, but she maintained her composure like she did when she was faced with a stressful situation on her job. Something that used to be hard to do, but the longer she was in the outside world, the easier it got.

But surprisingly it was harder to do now that she was back in Hunters Ridge, probably because here she reverted to her old self. Timid. Uncertain. Amish.

"I was never baptized, so putting me under the *Bann* is pointless."

"Eve!" Thomas scolded her. "Be respectful."

"You should think long and hard about housing such a negative influence," the bishop said in a gravelly, threatening voice.

Eve fisted her hands and forced herself to remain silent.

Leaning heavily on his cane, their elderly guest rose to his feet. Eve stood her ground as he got closer. She could smell the heat of his black suit. He waved his gnarled index finger inches from her face, and she resisted the juvenile urge to knock it away. "Aaron is a good man. You will not ruin his reputation again."

"Your grandson has issues, even if you turn a blind eye to it."

The bishop held up two fingers. "Two of my grandsons were here last night. I believe the other one is courting Mercy." He pivoted slowly and shot Thomas a knowing gaze. "I'd hate if that relationship fell apart. Your daughter seems happy."

"Roy is a *gut* man," Thomas said. "We'd be blessed to have him in our family."

Eve's mouth went dry. She met her brother's gaze and

could clearly see the concern in his eyes. She loved Mercy and didn't want to be held responsible for ruining her future, even if it was a future Eve couldn't imagine for herself.

Eve smiled tightly and feared her face would crack. "Please excuse me while I go change. I did promise my mother I'd behave while I was here." She turned and walked out of the house on shaky legs. If it weren't for her mother's health, she would have gotten back into her car and returned to Buffalo without so much as a backward glance.

CHAPTER 12

Later that evening, Dylan swung back by his former sister-in-law's house to drop off a gallon of paint. He hated to disappoint either of his nephews. Through the screen he could hear one of the boys making *pew-pew-pew* noises and the other one grunting and muttering, "You got me."

He paused at the door, often caught off guard by how such innocent moments slammed him back into his childhood, reminding him how he and Jacob used to spend entire afternoons in the fields behind their house playing games. Squaring his shoulders, Dylan stepped into the kitchen and made a show of reaching for his imaginary gun in his imaginary holster. "Hands up."

Both boys spun around, and instead of lifting their hands in surrender, ran with their heads down into his side and flung their arms around his waist and squeezed with all their might. Mason was the first to speak as he stepped back and yanked on the metal handle of the paint can. "Are we going to paint my room now?"

"Easy, buddy," Dylan said, releasing the handle to his four-year-old nephew. "It's heavy."

"I got it!" Mason's arm tugged down and he spun around and took an extra step to steady himself as the weight of the can sent him teetering off-kilter. "Mommmm!" he hollered. "Uncle Dylan's here." He set the can down with a clack on the kitchen linoleum. With the curiosity of a little boy inspecting an ant under a microscope, Mason fingered the orange dot on the metal lid, the small paint sample swiped there by the Amish clerk who mixed the color. Mason looked up with wide-eyed awe. "You got orange. That's just what I wanted."

"Of course, but we should probably double-check with your mom before we paint all four walls with it." He knew Tessa wouldn't care, but he needed the boys to remember that their mom was the one in charge around here, especially since they had become adept at getting whatever they wanted from their uncle.

Mason disappeared into the other room and returned with his new paintbrush. He chuckled at seeing the mangled bristles again. Tessa came into the room behind him. Her eyes brightened. "I didn't realize you were stopping by tonight."

"I felt bad we had to leave the hardware store without Mason's paint." He wanted the little guy to know he could count on his uncle. Always.

Tessa tipped her head, her long blonde ponytail swept over one shoulder. She looked the same as she did when the Kimble twins met her in the seventh grade. She had moved here from Buffalo when her father took over as plant manager of the cheese factory in town. He had since retired, but her family remained rooted in Hunters Ridge. Tessa and Jacob had been middle school sweethearts and started what they hoped would be their happily ever after.

Dylan wondered what Tessa would do if given a choice between the two Kimble boys. Would she still choose his brother? It was a strange question he asked himself every so often. It wasn't that he had some unrequited crush. It was more like wondering if she ever thought about the path not taken. Heaven knew, he went down that road himself, but not with Tessa. It was with the quiet Amish girl whom he got to know while pretending to love movies. Well, it wasn't that he hated movies. He just had more interest in Eve.

"Why didn't you bring your friend in earlier?" Curiosity and amusement laced Tessa's tone.

"I figured you had to get Mason to soccer practice."

"We did... Still, I would like to meet her." Tessa seemed to be studying him carefully.

Good thing he had long ago mastered his poker face, a very practical skill in his line of work. "I had to help Eve with a flat, and then Mason and I invited her to lunch."

"Eve?" Her eyes narrowed, as if she was trying to figure something out. The same serious expression he had seen too many times to count when his sister-in-law came to him worried about her husband. Dylan's brother.

He shook the thought away and focused on what was right in front of him. A trick he had learned after searching for a way to cope with his twin's senseless death.

"A friend?" Tessa said. "Does this happen to be the Amish girl you hung out with when you worked at the movie theater?"

Dylan jerked his head back in surprise that she knew.

Tessa waved her hand. "You know, your brother told me everything. And Eve isn't a very common name."

The thought of his brother alive and well and confiding in Tessa made him nostalgic for a time when they both seemed to have the world—their entire lives—ahead of them.

Youth was wasted on the young, and all that. "What did Jacob say?"

Delight flashed in her eyes. "You really want to know?" Her lips curved into a bold smile. "He said he thought you had a crush on an Amish girl."

Dylan wrinkled his face, as if the idea was ridiculous.

"Might explain why you turned down Rebecca Sanders when she asked you to her senior prom."

"I was not going to a high school prom when I was in college."

Tessa cocked an eyebrow.

"That's not why…" His protest died on his lips when he suddenly recalled disappointing Rebecca. He purposely picked up an extra shift at the theater prom night so that his excuse that he had to work would hold up.

"Whatever you say." She pulled out a chair and flopped down in it.

"Come on, Uncle Dylan, let's get busy." Mason stomped back into the kitchen and hoisted the paint can with a grunt.

"It's too late to start tonight. We'll get to it first thing in the morning if that's okay with your mom." He could swing by Eve's with her new tire after lunch. "I have a few days off this week."

Mason sought his mother's permission with puppy dog eyes.

"Yes, of course, tomorrow morning." Tessa leaned forward and placed her son's face between her palms and planted a kiss on his forehead. "Go and play with your brother and let your uncle and me chat."

Without having to be told a second time, Mason bolted into the other room. A moment later, the sound of cartoons floated into the kitchen. Tessa didn't like the boys to watch too much TV, but he suspected they knew a good opportunity when they saw one.

"Have you had dinner?" Tessa made like she was going to stand. "I can fix you something."

"No, thanks anyway." Tessa was good to him, and he in turn, tried to step up and fill the gaping hole his brother's death had left.

She got up and grabbed a beer from the door of the fridge and handed it to him. "How about a drink?"

He accepted the cold beer and they settled in at the kitchen table. He braced himself for Tessa's inquiry with a long pull on the bottle. He wiped his lips with the back of his hand, then said, "Yes, Eve is the same Eve I was friends with at the movie theater."

Tessa took a sip of her own beer and studied him carefully. "How long has it been?"

"I was still an undergrad. Seven years, I guess." He tapped his thumb in a rhythmic beat on the side of the bottle.

"And now she's calling you out of the blue? Whatever happened to her?"

"Both those questions have complicated answers." He felt himself smiling as Tessa leaned back in the chair, as if getting comfortable, and raising her eyebrows in an *I've got time* gesture.

"I don't know all the details. Only that she had a run-in with someone at her family farm last night and had to call the sheriff's department."

"And you showed up. Rather serendipitous." She eyed him skeptically.

I suppose it was. "Small town."

"True." She set her drink on the table. "Mason never mentioned her being Amish, so I take it she's left the community and she's home visiting."

"Yes, home for a visit. Her mom's sick."

"That's tough. So, your chance at catching up with her,"

she continued, "involved Mason?" She laughed. "I'm sure my son dominated the conversation. Sorry about that."

"Goodness, no. Having him there made it easier. Very casual."

"Glad to hear that. Are you going to see her again? I mean, while she's in town?" The way she asked suggested she didn't believe Eve would be a fleeting moment.

He lifted a shoulder. "I promised her that I'd bring a new tire to the house tomorrow. She can't keep driving around on the spare."

"Ah, sweet Dylan, always helpful."

The grating chatter from a commercial reminded him of the television and Eve's job. "Hey," he said, "you ever catch any of the local morning shows coming out of Buffalo?"

Tessa shook her head. "Nope. Can't remember the last time I watched something I wanted. Anytime that TV goes on, it's kids' programming. Why?"

"Eve said she works on a show in Buffalo."

"Interesting." Tessa seemed to consider it a moment longer. "Seems like a big leap from Amish to TV personality."

"Yeah, I think she started behind the scenes mostly." Dylan tried to imagine Eve's life in Buffalo and came up blank.

"Sounds like you need to get to know Eve better."

Dylan grimaced. "She won't be in town long."

Tessa leaned forward, resting her forearms on the table. "You're a great guy. It's about time you found someone." She picked up the beer bottle by the neck and slowly swirled it in circles on the smooth wood surface. "When you think of it, Buffalo isn't *that* far." Dylan's eyebrows drew down and he was about to come up with another excuse when Tessa added, "Before you get too busy for us, make sure you finish all my home improvement projects first." She laughed and quickly pushed away from the table and stood. If he hadn't been watching her, he might have missed the sadness that swept across her face and quickly disappeared.

"Want some chips?" She patted his shoulder on her way to the pantry, then paused with her back to him. "Dylan, you need to find your own happiness. Grab it while you can."

CHAPTER 13

*L*ater that night, Eve retreated to her bedroom after her mother had settled in. She left the roller blind up because she loved to watch the dramatic colors of the sky as the sun set over the fields. Grandma Gerty had lived a lifetime of going to bed early and rising even earlier. Her illness made her more tired. Hopefully the pain meds Eve had picked up in town would help her sleep better.

Eve wasn't anywhere ready to call it a day, so she propped up the pillow behind her on her twin bed and tried to focus on the novel on her Kindle. Since she wasn't connected to the grid, she figured it was another loophole when it came to technology that she could exploit.

Eve had started to read the same paragraph for the third time when her cell phone tucked in the bedside table whispered to her. She was trying to abide by the rules, but she hadn't realized how integral electronics were to her life. She slid out the phone and opened the note app and wrote: *swing by Dr. Gray's office and get Mom's files*. She'd have to take care of that before Wednesday. Thomas would probably lose his mind when she jumped in her car to go back into town. She was beginning to feel a little sheepish about not keeping her promise to her mother.

How did she ever manage to stay put on the farm for the first eighteen years of her life?

Eve tossed the phone down on the bed and picked up her Kindle again, her fingers growing twitchy for her laptop. Maybe she should publish the blog entry she had written and saved into draft. Perhaps it would help another person in her position. Her eyes moved to her closed bedroom door. Was it breaking the rules if no one knew?

Gott knew. How many times had she been told that as a child? A threat to make her obedient. Despite her wavering faith, *she* knew. And she had made a promise to her mother.

She picked up her e-reader, grateful for the backlit screen so she wouldn't have to struggle to read under the soft glow of the kerosene lamp. She laughed to herself and tried once again to concentrate on the page. She figured it was a matter of retraining her brain to focus.

Psst...

Eve lifted her head and glanced toward the window. Pinpricks of apprehension washed over her. Then anger. If Aaron Brenneman thought he could come here again and harass her, he had another think coming. Especially after the bishop, his grandfather, had personally defended him. Maybe she should grab her cell phone and record him. No, she had a better idea.

Eve slipped one foot then the other off the bed. The evening air had cooled the hardwood floor. She snuck to the closet and grabbed what Suze had dubbed "the beating stick," a metal bar they had decorated with reflective tape. She normally kept it in her trunk in case she ever broke down on a dark road, but she had moved it into the house after the first altercation on Sunday night. She and her friend Suze both obtained a crude weapon because they worried about all the bad things that could happen to a young woman left to her own devices.

Clutching the cool metal in her hand, she crept to the window, not that she actually thought Aaron would make it all the way into her bedroom, or that she'd have to use it. The beating stick was intended as a threat. That's all it had ever been.

"Leave now before I call the sheriff's department again."

"Eve. It's me." A soft voice had her lowering her arm. *Her niece.*

"Mercy? What are you doing? You almost gave me a heart attack."

"Come around to the front door and let me in. We need to talk." Before Eve had a chance to say no, Mercy turned and ran.

Eve tucked the weapon back into the closet and rushed through the sitting room to the porch where she found Mercy standing with her arms crossed over a long, white gown.

Apparently noticing her aunt's appraisal, Mercy said, "Easier to sneak back in if I'm already dressed for bed." She lifted the small tote bag in her arms. "I'd have to ditch this first."

"I really hope you have some of your mother's homemade brownies in there."

Mercy shyly tipped her head. "*Neh*, sorry. I could..." She glanced nervously over her shoulder. "I could go get you something."

"No, no. I was kidding." Eve held out her arm, inviting Mercy in. "Your mother was already gracious to bring us dinner tonight."

"I think she wanted to avoid more conflict. She doesn't like when you and my *dat* argue."

"Yeah, me neither." Eve lifted her finger to her lips. "Your grandmother is sleeping. Let's go in my room."

Her niece slipped past Eve. Her shoulders seemed to sag in relief, as if she had been bracing herself to sneak out to meet her aunt and had finally achieved her mission.

Once they were in her room—Eve perched on the bed cross-legged and Mercy in the rocking chair in the corner— she waited for her niece to tell her the reason for her visit.

Mercy rocked slowly and Eve had trouble reading her expression in the soft glow of the lamp. Eventually her niece opened up to her. "Do you ever regret your decision to leave Hunters Ridge?"

Eve ran her hand through her hair, mostly to gather her thoughts. She hadn't been expecting that. She had formulated an articulate response to exactly that question when someone anonymously had posed it to her in the comments section of her blog, but to have a beloved family member ask her? It held a lot more weight. Answering the same question asked by her niece, her brother's daughter, seemed more dangerous. What if Mercy decided to leave and it was her fault?

"You went for the jugular."

Mercy's forehead furrowed as if she didn't understand. She smoothed a hand over her hair still pulled back in a bun, but she wasn't wearing a head covering. She looked younger than her eighteen years in this light.

"You're asking a tough question." Eve tipped her head to catch Mercy's gaze. "Is that what brought you here?" Then realizing she was sidestepping the question, she said, "My biggest regret is that I had to leave my family. I had to leave you." She held out her hand and drew Mercy over to sit on the bed next to her. "And now I'm worried about Grandma Gerty. I've missed a lot of years with her." The familiar dread sloshed in her stomach. "Why do you ask?" She untucked her leg and shifted to study Mercy's face. "Is something wrong?" Her gaze drifted to the window. The hair on the back of her neck prickled to life and she stood, suddenly compelled to lower the blind.

"Is someone out there?" Mercy held her hand protectively on the bag she had brought with her.

"No, just a habit from living in Buffalo. I always draw the blinds at night."

"I suppose it didn't help that I led Aaron back here."

Eve's mouth grew dry. "Honey, that's not your fault. You had no idea he'd harass me. You had no idea Aaron and I have a negative history."

"You see…" Mercy reached into the tote and pulled out a book with a worn brown leather cover.

Eve's heart dropped. "Is that my…"

Mercy hugged the book to her chest, looking like she wanted to cry. "I did know."

Eve had assumed her journal had been tossed like all her other items. "Thomas told me he had burned everything from my hope chest." She had reached him on the phone in his small outbuilding where they did some potting. She'd wanted to let her family know she was safe. When she'd foolishly asked permission to return to pick up a few of her possessions, he'd cruelly given her the news. Part of her wondered if he had read her journals; another part was relieved that they were gone. Thomas's callousness had made it unnecessary for her to return to Hunters Ridge. Ever. She'd truly started over fresh, without the baggage of her past life.

If only her horrible memories were as easy to set flame to.

But it turned out Thomas had lied. Her favorite journal was being stroked by Mercy as if it were a fluffy stuffed animal. "After Grandpa Jebediah died and my family moved into the main house, I remember watching you write and write in it." She looked up sheepishly. "After you left, I heard *Dat* promising to destroy all your things, so I snuck into your room to rescue it. In case you came back."

The idea of eleven-year-old Mercy waiting for her to return made tears burn the back of her eyes. "I'm sorry I abandoned you without so much as a goodbye."

Mercy shrugged as if it was no big deal when it obviously was a very big deal. She extended the journal to her.

Eve swallowed hard. The smooth leather felt familiar, but its musty smell was what took her immediately back. "Did you read it?" *Of course she did.* She worried about how the events she wrote about could color a child's perception of her insular world. "You were so young. I hope I didn't confuse you."

"I didn't read it back then." Mercy lifted her chin and gently dragged a stray hair behind her ear. "You told me they were your private thoughts."

Eve had tried to impress upon her niece that she shouldn't go through her aunt's things, a very real possibility since they had shared the same house. "I appreciate that. But you said 'back then.'" She opened the journal up to a random spot and smoothed her hand across the page. What she wouldn't do to have a chat with the young woman with this neat penmanship. "You've read it more recently?"

"I didn't mean to betray your trust." Mercy lifted her chin; this time Eve detected a subtle quiver. Eve wanted to pull her into an embrace, but sadly the years separating them kept them apart still. Mercy continued, "I've been hanging around Roy Brenneman a lot."

Eve waited. Her heart thrummed loudly in her ears. The bishop had suggested her niece and Roy were courting.

"When Roy introduced me to his family, some of them asked me what relation you were to me." Mercy's tone hardened. "It wasn't in the way someone asks and then follows up

with, 'Oh, I went to school with her' or 'What a lovely girl.'"
Her niece's eyes grew watery. "I'm sorry, this must sound awful and I don't mean to hurt your feelings."

Eve turned toward her niece and said in the sincerest way she knew how, "You could never hurt my feelings." Thoughts at how the Brenneman family must have quizzed Mercy made long-buried anger bubble to the surface and threaten to explode.

"They were holding something back," Mercy said.

"I'm surprised they had any restraint." The bishop never hesitated to make his feelings known when it came to Aaron Brenneman and Eve Reist.

"I think maybe Roy defended me. Told me I was nothing like my aunt." She shook her head. "But that didn't make any sense to me. I loved you."

Eve squeezed her niece's knee. "And I love you, Bug." She used her niece's nickname for the first time since she had returned.

Mercy had enjoyed playing in the fields and digging up all sorts of insects and worms. Bug sounded cuter than Worm. Her heart warmed at the memory.

Eve squared her shoulders and met Mercy's gaze. Gone was her little niece, replaced by a young woman. "What do you want to know?" Eve took her clues from Mercy. She didn't want to overwhelm her, and she wasn't sure how much information she was emotionally ready to share with her sweet, innocent niece. How would it color Mercy's perception of her?

It already has.

"Maybe you could tell me what happened that night," Mercy said, her voice hitching.

CHAPTER 14

When Eve didn't respond right away, Mercy leaned forward as if to stand up. "I shouldn't have pried." She scratched her forehead. "I shouldn't have asked." Then her voice grew quiet. "They were your private thoughts." The poor girl was obviously conflicted.

Eve placed the journal on the bed next to her, allowing her fingers to linger on the smooth leather cover. She had poured her teenage heart out onto these pages. Could she really talk about these things? Her niece had given her an easy way out. But there really was no easy way out. "Please don't spend another minute worried that you've offended me. I'm not mad at you. I promise." She forced a smile despite the weight on her lungs. "I would have done the same thing if I were in your shoes, especially since I got up and left without saying goodbye. I'm impressed you held off until recently."

Eve watched her niece's face and didn't detect any deceit. Mercy truly had waited until the Brenneman family made her wonder about her missing aunt's character.

"I'm sure you could tell I was mad at Aaron." Eve waded into uncertain waters. How would Thomas feel if he knew she was filling his daughter's head with ideas on how much she hated the bishop's grandson? Oh, hate was such a strong word. Aaron Brenneman was such a vile person. Eve's gaze went to the blind covering the window, then back to Mercy. "Aaron was courting me. But almost from the beginning I had my doubts." She stared off into the middle distance, not seeing the sparsely decorated room, but instead reliving the events leading up to that fateful night. "He was mean, so mean. Especially when he was drunk."

"Roy claims he doesn't drink anymore," Mercy said.

Of course his cousin would defend him. And, of course, his cousin was very wrong. Eve dragged her gaze to her niece and didn't bother to remind her that Aaron had his fair share of whiskey—or, whatever his drink of choice now was—on Sunday night.

"One night," Eve started retelling her story, "on the way home from Sunday singing, he pulled his wagon over in a field. I was cold. I wanted to go home."

Mercy's bare foot moved in a rhythmic motion.

"But he wouldn't listen. He gave me a hug and told me he'd keep me warm." His wet, sloppy mouth blew hot on her neck. She shuddered at the memory she omitted from the retelling.

Eve had turned her focus to a knot in the hardwood floor, unable to look at her niece as she retold the tale she hadn't shared since she tried to defend herself to the bishop and a few of the elders. A wave of outrage drowned any remaining reservations.

Yes, my niece needs to hear this story. To learn to stick up for herself.

"He assaulted me." The Amish were a faithful people, but they were human. Some young people fooled around, but that wasn't this. "I told him to stop and he got angrier."

A quiet gasp escaped Mercy's lips.

"I managed to untangle myself from his grip and jumped out of his wagon. He chased me across the field. Fortunately for me, I had an advantage. I wasn't drunk. He stumbled and hollered after me. He was enraged. I never ran so fast. I finally reached a farm, but I didn't want to wake the family that lived there. If word got out, your father would be mad at me. How would it look?"

Since leaving the Amish, Eve had learned about sexual harassment and the right to say no. Something she never knew when she was a naive Amish girl on the cusp of adulthood. On the verge of marrying this creep.

Eve blinked a few times slowly and continued. "Instead of going to the main house, I ran into a barn. I scrambled up a rickety ladder to the loft and hid." She crossed her arms over her midsection and in the quiet, heavily shadowed room, she was suddenly back behind the damp hay bale, her breath coming out on a cloud of condensation on the cold November night. "I heard him hollering for me for the longest time."

"Did he hurt you?" The warm light reflected in Mercy's bright eyes.

"Not physically, but he damaged my reputation." Eve's mouth went dry at the memory, at the frustration of trying to get her side of the story across to unreceptive listeners. "Maybe if I had stayed quiet about what happened, people wouldn't have had a reason to attack me personally."

"Do you wish you didn't tell anyone?" Mercy's question was so sincere, Eve worried that perhaps her young niece had more on her mind than her aunt's checkered past. "You wrote in your journals that Aaron attacked you and that no one believed you." The fabric of her sleeping gown bunched up as Mercy ran her hands up and down her thighs. "Why did people believe him over you? Because his grandfather is the bishop?" she added, already knowing the answer.

"That was part of it." Eve's pulse whooshed through her ears. Did she want to share every detail of the story? She hadn't even written about it in her journal. In a way, by not writing it down, the memory—the good part, not the details that were used against her—was forever close to her heart. "Aaron used a friendship against me."

Realization brightened her niece's face. "*Were* you seeing an *Englisch* boy?"

"I had a friend." Her best friend. The admission even now stunned her. She had shared more about her life with Dylan Kimble than anyone before or since. "And someone told Aaron about it and he accused me of dating him." Aaron had used far worse terms than dating. "And after I refused Aaron's advances and he chased me down, he turned everything around on me. He claimed that I had slept with this outsider. He tarnished my reputation." Eve was surprised she was able to hold back the tears. The indignation all these years later still had the potential to reduce her to a puddle. "Did Roy tell you about that?" A ticking started in Eve's brain. Through the grapevine, Eve had learned Aaron's sister had started the rumor.

"Roy was with me when we saw you on the news, and he didn't say anything. But a few days later when he learned you were coming back to Hunters Ridge, he claimed you spread lies about Aaron. It made me think of your journal. That's when I read it."

"Do you think differently of me now?"

Mercy shook her head. "*Neh*. I think Aaron's not as *gut* as everyone claims."

Eve's heart warmed. "Thank you." It meant the world to her that she automatically took her side. Then, slightly embarrassed, she added, "You'd think that seven years later none of this would still matter to them."

"I suppose they know the truth and the truth always prevails."

Eve leaned over and gave her niece a tight one-armed hug. "How did you know the most perfect thing to say to me? No one believed me back then. The bishop has a lot of influence."

"My *dat* didn't believe you?" Mercy's voice shook.

"The problem is, I did meet someone in town weekly to watch movies. He was *Englisch*, but we were just friends. Aaron's sister apparently wasn't the only one who had seen us in the theater." She had been foolish to be so careless. "It gave more power to Aaron's story."

"I'm sorry. And I'm sorry I didn't tell Roy to stuff it when he started talking negatively about you. I didn't want to make him mad."

Alarm bells rang in Eve's head. "Does he hurt you?"

Mercy lowered her gaze and shook her head. "*Neh*, nothing like that." She sighed. "I suppose I'm a lot like Mem. I don't like conflict."

"Fair enough. Mercy..." She waited until her niece looked up. "You can tell me anything. Okay? I won't get mad." Eve would have done anything to have someone in her corner back then.

"I know." Mercy frowned. "Is that why you left the Amish?"

"It played a big role."

"If Aaron never attacked you"—her niece seemed to be putting the pieces together—"you might have stayed?" The tinge of nostalgia in Mercy's voice broke her heart.

Eve chose her words carefully. "We'll never know." She sighed. "Listen, I'm sorry I hurt you when I left. I never, ever meant to hurt you. If I'm being honest, I'm a firm believer that things work out, however painful."

"Like fate?" There was a hopeful twist to her tone that made Eve suspect once again that there was something more going on behind her niece's visit tonight.

Eve didn't want to get into a discussion about beliefs. The Amish would say *Gott* had a hand. The idea of some arbitrary fate or destiny would be offensive to most. So perhaps God had led her to this life as an outsider. Her brother would never acknowledge that. And as far as God, Eve supposed if He had, He might have guided her to return to her faith, which she hadn't. It was something she avoided discussing, afraid she'd find judgment for her choices like she had among the Amish. But that wasn't a conversation for now.

Eve brushed her fingers across the journal. "I can't recall how much I detailed in here." The emotions more than the events had always weighed heavily on her. "Did you want to ask me anything?" As much as Eve didn't want to talk about the months leading up to her departure from Hunters Ridge, she did want to clarify things for her niece, if necessary.

"No." Mercy paused a moment, then added, "Unless you need someone to talk to."

Eve smiled at the kind gesture. "I'd like to forget about it." Something she'd never be able to do. The events had shaped her. Defined her future. "The bishop told me that you and Roy are courting. He warned me that if I wasn't careful, things might not work out between you two."

A muscle in Mercy's jaw twitched, then stilled. "What if I told you I didn't care?"

Eve jerked her head back. "Mercy, if you don't want to go out with him, you can break it off. You're young."

"Some of my friends are already making marriage plans."

"Don't feel the pressure."

"Did you feel like you didn't have a choice with Aaron?"

Eve looked up and into the corner, giving it some thought. "Initially I liked him. I was flattered by the attention. He's handsome. His family is well respected. But he showed himself not to be who I thought he was."

"I know what you mean. Roy was fun at first. I liked hanging out with him, but now I'm not so sure he's the one I want to be with for the rest of my life." Mercy leaned over and picked up the tote bag and folded it, then folded it again, smoothing the fabric in her lap.

The fine hairs on the back of Eve's neck prickled to life. "Has Roy done something to hurt you?"

Mercy shook her head. "He's an okay guy. And *Dat* thinks I should marry him because he's the bishop's grandson."

The qualifier made Eve's stomach sink. That had been part of the reason no one believed her story...because Aaron was the bishop's grandson. "Since you're a young Amish woman, you'll have to do a lot of things you might not want to do—like housework, cooking, childrearing. But marrying someone you don't want to isn't one of them." Eve studied her niece's face, not sure she was able to read her expression. Eve could still see the sweet child she used to spend hours on end with. Eve flattened her hand on the journal. "You know more about me than anyone else."

Mercy dipped her head, seemingly contrite again.

Eve smiled. "I told you that it's okay. Please. I forgive you. But now you have to promise me something. Promise me you won't make any decisions you can't live with." Whatever they might be. *"Promise."* Eve nudged her niece's shoulder playfully when she didn't answer.

"Promise," Mercy whispered. She sniffed and stood abruptly, as if she had just realized she had overstayed her welcome. "I better go. I don't want my *dat* to know I slipped out."

Eve reached out and touched her hand. "You're a *gut* person, Mercy."

A thin line marred her niece's forehead, as if she thought the comment was odd. Eve was about to explain when a soft smile tilted the young woman's lips. She understood.

Or at least Eve hoped she did. Eve would have done anything to have someone reassure her that she wasn't a bad person.

Even now.

CHAPTER 15

The elevator doors whooshed open and Eve and her mother stepped out into the lobby of the downtown hospital. Her mother had been fidgeting with her apron with trembling hands through the entire appointment with the oncologist. Eve had never seen her mother this far out of her element. Maybe this had been a bad idea, after all. Maybe she should have let her live out the rest of her days in Hunters Ridge without the constant doctor visits and potential treatment that would make her sicker than the disease.

Don't get ahead of yourself. She still needs a biopsy.

Maybe Eve shouldn't impose her will on someone else.

"We could get something to eat?" Eve asked hopefully. She would have loved to take Mem to her favorite burger stand by the lake.

"I'm not very hungry." Grandma Gerty adjusted her tote bag on her arm. Eve had encouraged her to bring her knitting to make the time pass, but her mother had been too nervous to even touch it.

Eve held the door open and as they stepped outside, one of those rare, hot, sticky August days in Buffalo enveloped them. They sidestepped the valets waiting to collect the cars of the patients who preferred that convenience. Eve liked easy in-and-out access in the parking garage across the street.

Eve tipped her head, studying her mother, remembering how uncomfortable it was to wear plain clothing in this heat. "If you're not feeling well, I can go get the car and come pick you up here." She had been grateful Dylan replaced her tire, making the trip into Buffalo less of a concern. And he had done it quickly so that her brother hadn't protested his presence on the farm. "Stay here. I'll be right back," Eve added when Mem seemed to be frozen with indecision. Perhaps the doctor's suggestions had been overwhelming.

Her mother's gaze scanned all the people waiting for their vehicles. Many of them were eyeing her with curiosity, something Eve remembered all too well. "I'd rather go with you," she said softly. They stopped at the curb and waited for a few cars to pass on the busy medical corridor. "Will we have to return here?"

Eve looked both ways and they hurried across the street. "The doctor needs you to have some tests to see what we're dealing with. If it is cancer, they'll come up with a treatment plan. Remember the information she gave us about the MRI?" Eve kept flicking gazes in her direction as they navigated the sidewalk.

"Oh," her mother said, "I don't know about that." She had been consistent in one thing: her reservations about treating her potential breast cancer after watching her older sister go through it.

"I'll be with you the entire time," Eve said, trying to bolster her mother's deflated mood.

"But you have a job you'll have to get back to."

"Let me work that out." For once Eve was grateful for her

early morning job. In theory, it would free her up to run back and forth to Hunters Ridge. She'd make it work.

"I'll discuss it with Thomas." Eve heard a hint of resignation in Grandma Gerty's tone, as if she had already decided to use her eldest son as an excuse.

"Please, Mem. We need to explore all the options. I'm here. You don't have to bother Thomas." She sensed her mother formulating a protest, so she said, "Can we take it as it comes? Trust *Gott* that He has blessed this doctor with the smarts to help you."

Her mother pinched her lips and nodded ever so slightly. Eve felt a hint of regret at browbeating her. She knew she didn't like conflict and would probably agree to anything at the moment to stop the discussion.

They entered the garage on the opposite side of the street, took one flight up, and emerged onto the heavily shadowed second floor. Eve blinked a few times as her eyes adjusted from the bright summer day. Her mother paused, slightly stooped, sucking in air. Eve touched her mother's back. "Are you okay?" Eve glanced around. They was parked a few rows over. "Stay here. I'll get the car."

Her *mem* straightened and pressed a shaky hand to her chest. "*Neh, neh.*" Eve wasn't sure if the fear she saw on her mother's face was due to her health or the thought of being left alone here.

"Okay, okay, we'll walk a little more slowly." Eve slipped her hand through the crook of her mother's arm.

The heat released the scent of the laundry soap and took Eve immediately back to her childhood chore of hanging the heavy, wet laundry on the clothesline. When Eve got her first apartment, she relished the convenience of the in-unit washer and dryer. It was like magic. She never understood how her *Englisch* friends could complain about doing laundry when it virtually meant stuffing clothes into a machine and pulling them out clean. Part of her figured the bishop didn't allow electricity because he didn't have to do the laundry. She knew it wasn't as simple as that, but that was how it felt sometimes.

"We're almost there." Eve had slid a hand into the side pocket of her purse to grab the key fob when something caught her attention out of the corner of her eye. A flush of dread washed over her, chilling her warm skin. She released her mother's arm and spun around, effectively putting herself between the stranger and her mem.

"Eve?" her mother asked, obviously sensing her distress. "Eve?"

"Stay behind me."

"Excuse me, excuse me," the man said as he continued his advance, his shoulders forward and his steps heavy. He had a Buffalo Bills cap pulled low on his forehead, hiding his features.

Eve held up her hand. "Can I help you?" A smile wavered on her lips, partially from her conditioning as a child to be polite, part of her worry about offending a fan.

"No, I wanted to..." He grabbed her arm and twisted, his bony fingers digging into her flesh.

A pain shot up into her shoulder and adrenaline surged in her veins, making it hard to think clearly. She immediately realized she had missed an opportunity to defend herself before he snatched her. He kept his head dipped so she couldn't see anything but his snarled lip and his crooked teeth.

"Get away!" she commanded and tried to wrestle her arm free and simultaneously stomp on the insole of his foot. A pain shot up her heel and he didn't seem to flinch. Somewhere outside her periphery of awareness she could hear her mother repeating her name.

"Eve! Eve!" She wanted nothing more than to reassure her frightened mother, but she couldn't.

The man pushed Eve and she scrambled back before losing her footing and crashing down on her hip between her car and a black van. *Oh my goodness, I'm going to be kidnapped and my mother—*

She couldn't complete the thought. The man jumped on her and all the breath rushed out of her in a whoosh, startling her. He was fast. He landed a hard, stinging punch to her face, then grabbed her arms and pressed them against the cement over her head. His dark eyes held menace, yet something even darker lingered in their depths.

He's enjoying this. She bucked, trying to throw him off. The gravel bit into the back of her hands.

"Oh, you're a fighter." He leaned in and licked her cheek.

Eve's stomach lurched.

"Get off me!" she gritted out. "Get off."

"It'd be a shame if that pretty face got messed up." He let go of one hand and reached behind him.

His first mistake.

Adrenaline raging through her, she lashed out and her fist connected with cartilage. The crunch was oddly satisfying. Something metal clattered against the ground.

The man's hand flew to his nose, blood spurted out. "You...!" He muttered an expletive.

"*Rug! Rug!* Stop! Stop!" her mother yelled, winding up and whacking him with her canvas bag, further sending him off-balance.

Eve dug her heels into the cement and scurried out from under her attacker. While he was still bent over clutching his nose, she kicked him, her heel making a solid connection with the side of his head. His baseball cap flew off revealing sweaty, matted hair. He stumbled back, then getting his bearings, he spun around and bolted, disappearing in the same direction as he had come.

"Eve, are you okay?" Her mother stood frozen, all the color having drained out of her face. Eve wondered if she should rush her back into the hospital.

"I'm fine. I'm fine." Eve placed her hand gently on her mother's back. She drew in a few gulping breaths. "I'm perfectly fine. Are you okay?"

"*Yah, yah.* That man tried to stab you." Her mother's chest heaved in and out.

"What?" Eve absentmindedly wiped the bits of gravel from the back of her hands.

A young woman approached and gestured to them with her cell phone, and her gaze kept flicking toward the stairwell. "I saw what that guy did. Oh my gosh. Did he hurt you? He nearly plowed into me in the stairwell."

"I'm fine." Eve nodded. "Can you do me a favor and call 911?"

"Of course." The woman slid her finger over the screen, then lifted the phone to her ear.

"Tell them we're in the parking garage across from the hospital. Second floor." Eve didn't want the police to have to search for them. And she needed to get Grandma Gerty home as soon as possible. "Come on, sit down." She directed the key fob at the car. A high-pitched chirp echoed in the concrete space. She opened the passenger door and helped her mother get in. "I need to report this, then I'll take you home."

Mem nodded, her empty expression radiating her shock.

Leaving the door open for air, Eve walked between the car and the van where she had been attacked. The stranger's assurance that the police were on the way was reinforced by the sound of sirens in the distance. "Thank you," Eve said, relief making her knees feel weak. "I don't want to hold you up."

"I'd be happy to stay and give a statement." Something in the woman's expression shifted, and Eve found herself bracing for what inevitably would come next. "You're Evelyn Phoenix." A statement, not a question.

"I am." She smiled tightly.

"Um, do you think I could have a selfie with you?"

Reflexively Eve ran her hand over her hair and the woman shook her head.

"I'm sorry. That wasn't cool. Not now anyway." The woman glanced at her phone, then lowered it to her side. She pointed in the general direction of Eve's face and made an exaggerated grimace. "You're going to have to wear heavy makeup to hide what's sure to be a huge shiner."

Eve touched her cheekbone gingerly. "Yeah, I guess." Then she forced a smile. "I appreciate your understanding." Eve knew that if she was rude, she might be reading about her reputation on some social media site. How had she ever ended up as a mini-celebrity of sorts?

The woman glanced toward the car. "Are you doing a feature on the Amish?" She leaned in conspiratorially. "I work in accounts receivable at the hospital, and I've had to deal with them from time to time. They're fascinating." Her eyes grew bright. "Do you know they don't have health insurance?"

"Um..." Eve searched her mind for a way to spin this. She had always kept her Amish background separate from her life in Buffalo. Relief surged through her when she heard the sirens growing louder.

The woman flung her hand in her direction. "Why am I telling you? You're the reporter." The chatty woman answered her own question. Eve had no reason to correct her.

The sound of an engine roared in the confines of the ramp. The tires of a patrol car squealed around the corner. The officer parked and climbed out. "What happened here?"

Eve allowed the woman to give her account while Eve bent over and inspected under the van. What appeared to be a pocketknife rested under the back tire. A shudder scurried down her body. That was what must have made the clacking sound. He lost it when she hit him.

"Ma'am."

Eve looked up, sensing it wasn't the first time the officer had called out to her. "There's a knife there. The attacker dropped it."

The officer picked it up, careful to preserve fingerprints.

After he took their statements and accepted Eve's refusal to get checked out at the hospital, she climbed behind the wheel of the car and turned to her mother. "I suppose this didn't help my case." The hint of humor in her tone was a coping mechanism that was lost on her terrified mother. She'd never agree to come back to Buffalo for treatment.

Her mem's hand fluttered around the hollow of her neck. "Please, take me home."

CHAPTER 16

Eve and Grandma Gerty rode back to Hunters Ridge mostly in silence. She had convinced her mother to let her pick up takeout so they could relax at home with dinner instead of joining her brother's large, boisterous family. Her mother stayed in the car and Eve did a quick check of her face in the rearview mirror before going into the diner. A bruise had blossomed on her cheek from where her attacker's fist had connected. She shuddered to think what would have happened if she hadn't knocked the knife out of his hand.

"I'll be right back." Eve hopped out of the vehicle, finding herself looking around, as if her head was on a swivel. She forced her shoulders down. She wondered how long until her nerves stopped buzzing and her stomach stopped aching.

Relax, I'm in Hunters Ridge now. I'm safe.

She smiled at a passing Amish woman who quickly looked down and away. Inwardly Eve rolled her eyes. Apparently she couldn't go anywhere without being recognized, but for very different reasons. Had the attack this afternoon been random? Her gut said no. She feared her overzealous fan—she liked to imagine it was only one deranged individual—had tracked her down. The police officer told her they'd do their best to find the guy, but there had been a rash of assaults in the area. She explained about her history and the officer made a note, but Eve wasn't hopeful.

Initially, she had planned to give Suze a quick call now that she was out of earshot of her mother, but changed her mind as she approached the diner. She didn't want to be overheard. By anyone. Hopefully she'd get reception back on the farm, and she could reach out to her friend in Buffalo later tonight.

As soon as she entered the restaurant, a young waitress approached with a friendly smile. "Just one?"

"I came in for pickup."

"Sure, Eve, right?" The waitress pointed to herself. "I took your order." She tipped her head toward the counter. "Just holler to Micky. He'll drop the fries now so they're fresh."

"Thanks," Eve said, more upbeat than she felt. She had hoped to dip in and out of the diner quickly. She waved to the man she suspected was Micky, and he assured her that her order would be "right up." So Eve slid onto a counter stool and drummed her fingers on the chipped Formica. Then, suddenly getting that creepy-watched vibe, she adjusted her hair to hide the tender bruise on her cheek.

"Hey, Micky."

Eve turned toward the familiar voice and butterflies flitted in her stomach. "Hey, Dylan," she said, now even more self-conscious.

"Hey, yourself." Dylan took a step toward her, paused, and seemed to be scrutinizing her closely. "What happened here?" He reached out, gingerly touching her cheek. The concern in his eyes melted her heart. But his compassionate gaze quickly hardened. "Was it Brenneman?" he asked, his deep, gruff voice rolling over her.

Eve glanced around the dining room where everyone seemed to be focused on their meals before turning her attention back to Dylan. "No, not Brenneman. I was..." She bit her lower lip, carefully choosing her words. "I was mugged in a parking garage in Buffalo."

"When you went in for the appointment?" He frowned. "Are you okay?"

Eve waved him off. "I'm fine. And my mother's fine. But wish me good luck getting her back to the city for treatment." Her attempt at humor fell flat. Again.

"Did you file a police report?"

"Of course—"

"Order for Eve?" Micky pointed at her then spun the silver order wheel sending the little white pieces of paper fluttering. She nodded in confirmation. "Give me a few more minutes."

"Thanks." Then to Dylan: "The officer told me there had been other attacks in the area."

"I'm going with you next time." He nodded, as if it were a fact. "Did you get a good look at him?"

Eve closed her eyes and drew in a deep breath. The memory of the attacker's menacing eyes made her stomach hurt. "I gave all the information to the local police." She reached out and brushed her hand across his, then pulled it away, as if she had touched something hot. "I'm tired. I'm hungry. I don't want to talk about it."

"Okay, okay." Dylan was obviously not done with it. "Mind if I stop by the farm? Discuss this with you? I need to make sure you're safe." Before she had a chance to answer, he added, "What time would be good?"

She smiled tightly in resignation. "My mother usually retires for the night by nine. Come over then."

"Here you go. Hot off the grill." The cook had emerged

from the kitchen and planted a white paper bag complete with grease stains in front of her.

"Thank you." She shifted her hip and dug into her back pocket where she had stuffed some cash.

Dylan gently placed his hand on her arm. "I'll get it."

"Thanks." She was too tired to protest. "I guess that means I'll get next time."

Half his mouth quirked into a handsome grin. "Count on it. And Eve…"

She turned slowly to face him.

"Drive safely. I'll see you later tonight."

∼

Eve cleaned up the wrappers from their takeout, reassured to see some color had returned to her mother's face. She made them both tea. "Are you feeling a bit better?"

Grandma Gerty took a sip and nodded. "It's nice to be home."

Eve set her mug down. She had so much to discuss, but tonight probably wasn't the time. Mem wouldn't be agreeable to anything since she was obviously still upset about the attack. *Will she ever get over it?* "Would you like one of Katy's brownies?" Eve asked.

"No, *denki*." Her mother fidgeted with the ceramic mug handle. "Please come home for *gut*."

"Mem, you know I have a life in Buffalo. And it's not always like that." The feebleness of her response echoed in her ears.

"I heard that woman in the parking garage call you Evelyn Phoenix. Is that your name now?"

A ticking started in her head and her mouth grew dry. "A lot of people take what they call a stage name."

"What's wrong with your given name?" Her mother

regarded Eve with a look of disappointment, an all-too-familiar expression that filled her with shame.

Eve decided to be honest. "Reist is a common Amish name. I wanted to start over."

"Are you ashamed of who you are?" Grandma Gerty's hesitant tone softened the harshness of the question and broke Eve's heart at the same time.

"No, I'm not ashamed of who I was. But I'm someone different now. I like my life." Eve gingerly touched her tender cheek, feeling like she was overselling it.

"So much danger there." Her mother swallowed hard. "That man today…" Tears brimmed in her mother's eyes and her lower lip quivered.

"I'm so sorry you had to…" Eve let her words trail off. "I refuse to live my life afraid."

"You wouldn't have to be frightened here." Her mother's gaze drifted to the window and the farm beyond. "It's peaceful."

Not always. But she kept her thoughts to herself.

"I should have listened to you." Her mother had a faraway look in her eyes and Eve waited her out. "You told me you didn't want to marry Aaron and I pushed. I pushed." Regret made her voice tremble. "I thought you'd be happy with him because he's the bishop's grandson. Everyone insisted he was a *gut* man."

Eve bit back a frustrated scream. How many times had she heard that Aaron was a good man because of his relationship to the bishop?

"But there are a lot of other decent men here." Her mother pressed on. "You're still young."

Eve wrapped her hands around her mug and focused on the smooth feel of it. "I know I agreed to dress plain while I'm here"—something she hadn't actually honored yet because she had been running errands—"and you've suggested I might find a husband, but I have no interest in staying here. Not like you want me to."

"But..."

Eve rubbed her temples. "It wasn't a matter of not liking Aaron." Not entirely.

Her mother bowed her head. Frizzy hair haloed her white bonnet much like it did after she had spent a day bent over a wash basin. "Was he really that bad?"

Eve gritted her teeth and felt the heat of anger warm her cheeks.

Her mother must have sensed her mood and frowned. "I'm sorry, I wished I would have listened to you. Your father used to say, 'If you give them an inch, they'll take a mile.' I was trying to be stern with you kids." Anguish laced her tone and made the back of Eve's eyes prickle.

Eve reached out and took her mother's hand. "None of what happened was your fault."

"I could have talked to Thomas. Told him not to be so hard on you. We were all so worried about how things looked in the eyes of the church."

Eve's heart broke for her mother. The incident today must have brought a lot of old feelings to the surface. "I love you. You are a wonderful mother. You need to forgive yourself." She decided not to get into all the details on how Aaron had attacked her. It was old news.

"I did the best I could."

Eve stood and hugged her mother's shoulders. "I love you."

Her mother patted her hand. "I love you, too." She struggled to stand, steadying herself on the table for a moment before reaching with a trembling hand for her cane. "I'm going to knit for a bit before calling it a night."

Eve considered making a crack about her mother slugging the attacker with her knitting bag, but decided the moment had passed. A quiet ringing sounded from deep in her purse. "I'll get that."

"All the distractions," her mem muttered and Eve smiled to herself, happy to have the woman she knew back.

Eve snagged her phone then slipped outside. "Hey, Suze."

"Oh my goodness, I heard what happened. Are you okay?"

Eve absentmindedly walked around the back of the house to the swing her father had hung on the tree another lifetime ago. "How?"

"Carol," they said in unison.

Of course word would have gotten back to the station about one of their reporters getting attacked in the parking garage, and *of course* Carol would be in the know.

"Are you okay?" Suze asked. An air of excitement made the inquiry seem less sincere.

"Yeah, fine." If one more person asked her how she was, she was going to scream.

Eve hooked one arm around the rope and toed the dirt, lazily moving back and forth on the swing. "My poor mother will be terrified to return to Buffalo."

"Oh, I'm sorry. I know how reluctant she was to go in the first place." A tapping sounded over the line, and Eve imagined her friend fidgeting with a pencil like she always did when they were producing a story behind the scenes.

"I miss the days of being anonymous."

"I wonder if it was the same fan that's been harassing you? Like, how weird would that be?"

Eve sighed. "How would he have known..." She lifted her eyes to the stars. "There's no way of knowing for sure at this point, but I'm tired. It's been one bad thing after another."

"It'll calm down."

"You think?" Eve asked, adjusting her grip on the rough swing rope.

"Sure! Besides, your promotion is worth it, right? Gotta weigh the pros and cons."

"True," she said, for lack of anything better to say. How could she tell her friend that she was having second thoughts about her new job in light of all the stuff going on in her life? A full-time job on camera would only make her more visible to unstable people who thought she owed them something. It would sound ungrateful, especially since both Suze and Carol had treated her like part of their family and had a hand in how far she had come.

"How did your mom's doctor's appointment go?" Suze asked.

"Good. We have to start with the biopsy which is scheduled for next week. If I can get her back to the hospital."

"I'll keep her in my prayers." Suze's words were wrapped around a yawn.

The sound of a vehicle pulling up the lane drew Eve's attention. Her traitorous heart started racing. *Dylan.* "I have to go, Suze."

"Have an exciting barn raising to go to?"

Eve ignored the joke. No wonder she wanted to hide her Amish roots. It was simpler to start fresh as Evelyn Phoenix. "Night. I'll talk to you soon."

She hopped off the swing and slid the phone into her back pocket. She walked around to the front of the house and found Dylan approaching.

"Hey there," she said.

"There you are." He took a step back and a wide smile brightened his handsome face. *Oh, I'm done for.*

Suddenly, the weight of the day lifted from her chest and she could breathe again.

Eve wasn't so sure that was a good sign.

CHAPTER 17

Dylan noticed Eve coming around the side of the house as he was about to climb the steps to her mother's home. He tucked his fingers in the front pockets of his jeans and pulled his shoulders back. *Man, she looks good.*

"Would you mind taking a drive?" She slid her phone into her back pocket and seemed to be anxious to get away from here. He imagined her presence alone was a source of conflict on the Amish farm.

"Sure." He turned on his heel and opened the passenger's side door for her. The dome light flowed out, casting the bruise on her cheek in darker shadow. He lifted his hand and stopped short of brushing his thumb across her smooth skin. "Looks like it hurts."

She shook her head dismissively. The sound of the screen door slamming in its frame sounded across the yard. "Let's go. Let's go." She yanked the seat belt across her and clicked it into place.

Dylan jogged around to the driver's side. He waved casually to her brother who stood with his fists on his hips, watching them.

After he buckled in and made a three-point turn to get back out on the road, he said, "Thomas doesn't look happy with you."

Eve let out a long sigh. "Ah, he can get in line behind everyone else who has a problem with me."

Dylan cut her a sideways glance. "It'll get better."

She laughed woefully. "You promise?" Then she quickly held up her hands. "No, don't make promises you can't keep."

When Dylan searched his brain for something to say that didn't sound trite, he came up empty so he changed the subject. "You like ice cream?"

"Ha! Does anyone *not* like ice cream?"

Dylan drove into town and they both ordered hot fudge sundaes at the seasonal ice cream stand that was usually teaming with tourists during the day. By the time they arrived—shortly before closing—there was no line. After they got their sundaes, they walked to the edge of Main Street and to the quiet park. They sat on opposite sides of a picnic bench under the soft glow of the white twinkling lights strung up on the gazebo.

Eve sighed heavily, as if she had the weight of the world on her shoulders. She tipped her head back and looked up at the sky. "This is pretty."

Dylan took the opportunity to study her face. "Sure is." He dragged his spoon through his soft serve vanilla. He wished this moment could last forever. "You sure you're okay?"

"Can we *please* talk about something else?" The exasperation was evident in her voice as she poked at her ice cream with her red plastic spoon. "At least until I'm done eating?"

"Sure." He didn't mind. He hoped to get to know her all over again, so he asked, "Are you still writing?"

"You remembered." She averted her gaze and a pink blush colored her cheeks. The bruise under her eye had darkened.

"I always wanted to write stories like the ones we watched at the movies." She shrugged. "I could have never done that if I stayed." Then she laughed, seemingly at herself. "I haven't since I left either." She lifted her spoon to her mouth, then lowered it. "Turns out, it takes a lot of discipline to write on a regular basis. I studied journalism in college and thought I'd write articles at least, but then I ended up in broadcasting. Not uncommon for a journalist, but not what I had planned."

"But it seems you've done well for yourself."

"Sure." She didn't sound convinced. "I feel out of place much of the time, but everyone needs a job, right?"

"You can change course." He hoped she didn't take his comment as self-serving.

"It pays the bills." She smiled. "We both know that life doesn't always turn out as planned." Then as if suddenly remembering, she dipped her head and said, "I'm sorry. Jacob's death had to be a horrible blow to your family."

"It was. I couldn't leave my nephews."

"You're a good guy." She took a bite of ice cream and watched him closely. "Besides catching the bad guys, what have you been up to since our hot dates in the back of the theater?" There was something dark in her humor.

"Hot dates, huh?" Dylan laughed.

"If only people knew." Her brow twitched.

"What do you mean?"

Eve shook her head and seemed to sober. "I shouldn't have brought it up."

"Please..." He reached across the table and stopped short of covering her hand. "What's going on?"

"You mean, why are my brother and the bishop still angry with me?"

He tilted his head. "You can talk to me. What happened? Did Aaron have something to do with it?"

"Aaron is a major creep." She ground out the words.

"You told me he has a history of getting drunk and harassing you."

Eve nodded slowly and she wrapped her arms around herself. "The final straw was when I refused his advances one night. We were alone in his wagon. I got away and he chased me. I hid in a stranger's barn loft."

Dylan's heart sank. "Did he...did he hurt you?"

"No, no. Not physically."

"Why did the community support him and not you? He was drunk and he was *wrong*." From working in law enforcement he already knew the Amish didn't always play by the same rules. "Was it because he's the bishop's grandson?" He searched her face.

"Partly..." She stood and stepped out of her side of the picnic table and tossed her half-eaten ice cream in the trash can. Facing away from him, she said, "Can we walk?"

"Sure, sure..." Dylan disposed of his empty container and placed his hand on the small of her back. "Let's walk."

They strolled in companionable silence down Main Street, past the diner, a vacant building, and the hardware store. It reminded him of the bedroom he promised his nephew he'd paint that he kept postponing. He turned to watch a horse and buggy pass. Mr. Yoder tipped his broad-brimmed hat in greeting. Dylan had helped him corral his cows last week when they escaped a broken section of fence.

"No one here will support me over Aaron. I want to forget it. I need to keep the peace long enough to help my mom." Eve slowed and turned to face him. "Okay?"

Dylan studied her eyes. "If he bothers you again, I'm going to do something about it."

Eve looked up at him shyly. "Why haven't I met a guy like you in Buffalo?"

Dylan reached out and tucked a strand of hair behind her

ear, leaving a warm trail of tingles under his touch. "I'm glad you didn't."

∽

Eve lifted her hand to her cheek, momentarily touching the place where Dylan's fingers had been. She glanced around, making sure no one was in earshot. She had to clear the air completely. Tell him what had been holding her back.

"There was another reason I left Hunters Ridge," Eve said.

"Oh..." Dylan fixed his gaze on hers, and she faltered for a moment. He was such a good guy that she didn't want to make him feel guilty.

"I probably should let it go."

"Tell me," he insisted. "What is it?"

Eve pressed her lips together, gathering her thoughts. "After Aaron was reprimanded for getting drunk that night I had to hide in the barn, he apologized profusely. But when I tried to explain to my brother how Aaron had been..." She searched for the right words, words she still struggled to find even now with her current maturity, something she lacked as a naive Amish girl. "Aggressive. How he had attempted to..." Eve dipped her head and let her hair fall in a curtain, hiding her face. "Thomas told me I must be mistaken."

"Your own brother?" Eve detected more than a touch of anger in Dylan's tone.

A whisper of defensiveness stiffened her spine. "He means well." Then she closed her eyes, hearing herself. Would she ever be able to shed the Amish girl she once was? "The reason I didn't stand my ground was because the elders confronted me with rumors I couldn't defend myself against. When I came forward with accusations against Aaron, they turned it around on me. They told me I needed to confess to dating an *Englisch* man. That others had seen me in the back of the theater." There was no mistaking what that alluded to.

Dylan's face grew slack then his eyes hardened. "Are you serious? We were only friends. We talked. It was innocent." A vein pulsed in his head. "There was nothing inappropriate."

"That's how things go." Her tone was resolute.

"Wait, you didn't defend yourself?"

His rightful indignation made her smile. "How? Aaron's own sister had seen us. I couldn't deny I had been there—someplace I should have never been anyway."

"You left because of me?"

"It was so much bigger than you. Someone else came forward and said that you were a known drug user, and by association I, too, was guilty."

"My twin brother..." Eve hated the devastation in his voice.

"It had to be. I didn't put it together until you told me he had died of a drug overdose. I shouldn't have shared this with you. I understand how painful your brother's death was."

"No, no, I'm glad you did." He scrubbed a hand over his face and sighed. "I'm so sorry."

"None of this is your fault. I wasn't happy here. That entire sequence of events propelled me to make a decision I might have been afraid to make otherwise." She slowed and sat down on the brick ledge of the window on an abandoned building with a big *For Rent* sign. "I think that's the first time I actually voiced that in so many words. Yeah, the worst night of my life changed the direction of my life. But in the end, I'm where I need to be." *Mostly.*

"I wish you would have come to me." Dylan sat down next to her on the windowsill.

"I couldn't. This was something I had to figure out for myself. And I'm still working things out." She tapped her feet on the pavement. "Probably a little deeper than your usual dates." She laughed.

"So this was a date?" He mirrored her laugh.

"Goodness, I've missed you." Her heart started beating hard. "I've never been able to talk to anyone like I was able to talk to you." She wrapped her hand around the brick ledge between them and leaned over and nudged his shoulder. "The more time that passed, I figured I had been romanticizing our chats."

Dylan placed his hand over hers and laced their fingers. "Absence makes the heart grow fonder."

"Yeah..." she said with a faraway quality to her voice. "It does." She leaned over and rested her cheek on his shoulder. "It really does."

Eve slapped at a mosquito buzzing around her arm. Dylan stood and extended his hand out to hers.

"Come on. Let's go."

She slid her hand into his and he pulled her up. She couldn't deny the attraction flitting in her stomach and she didn't know what to do with it. They didn't have a future now, any more than they did back then. They both had other priorities. They lived in different places.

When they arrived at his truck, he reached around her to open the passenger door and she paused to face him. "Thanks for this."

"What?" He stepped closer.

"Getting me out of the house." The warmth of his body close to hers radiated even though there was still room for the Holy Ghost. Inwardly she smiled at the image. Apparently, you could take the girl out of Hunters Ridge, but you couldn't take Hunters Ridge out of the girl. "I need to be here for my mom, but it hasn't been easy. This has been a nice break."

"It has." He lingered in front of her and her heart jackhammered in her chest.

When he didn't make his move, she stepped closer to him and placed her hands on his chest. Electricity shot through her palms as she slid them up and around his neck. She got up on her tiptoes and planted a kiss on his lips. Tentatively. His hand slid around her back and pulled her against his solid frame. Encouraged, she deepened the kiss. He tasted of ice cream and summer nights and long-ago conversations in the back of the movie theater.

Reluctantly, Eve broke the kiss and came down on her heels. Her entire body was on fire.

Dylan cupped her cheek and gently tangled his fingers in her hair. "You don't know how long I've wanted to do that."

Eve tilted her face into his warm touch. "Why doesn't such a great guy like you already have a girl?"

"I guess I've been waiting for you to return."

Eve closed her eyes and laughed. "You're one smooth talker."

Dylan gently took her chin and encouraged her to look up at him. His expression grew somber. "I know you have a lot going on, and I don't want to scare you away, but I'd really like to get to know you again."

Eve wanted to protest. Tell him she had been burned by love, or what she thought was love. And had too much going on in her life. But right here, right now, she only wanted this. "Okay," she whispered.

Dylan smiled brightly and planted a soft kiss on her lips. He reached behind her and opened the truck door. He politely waited until she climbed in and he closed the door. She watched him jog around to the driver's side with a certain lightness in his step. Her heart fluttered, then she swallowed hard.

This could only end in heartbreak. Again.

CHAPTER 18

The next morning, Eve woke up feeling excited which was quickly tempered by an undercurrent of uncertainty and indecision. She silently opened her mother's bedroom door to check on her and was reassured by the steady up-and-down of her mother's breaths. Pulling the door closed, she made coffee and stepped outside to escape the dawdy haus that with each day was feeling more confining. She would have done anything to come home and share the details of her date, but that wasn't the kind of relationship she and her mother had. Well, unless it was an Amish man who was courting her.

Is that what Dylan is doing? The idea warmed her heart, even if it was impractical. Like seven years ago, they were in completely different places in their lives.

Across the yard, her sister-in-law was hanging laundry. The twins toddled around underfoot, occasionally stopping to tip the basket or grab onto their mother's leg. Eve couldn't help but watch the scene unfolding in front of her, realizing that was the life she had been meant to live. She wondered, not for the first time, that perhaps, in a convoluted way,

Aaron had done her a favor of sorts by forcing her hand. Otherwise she might be hanging the wash right now or tending to young children.

Katy stretched to pin the corner of one of her husband's shirts to the line. She'd turned to reach into the basket when she paused and waved. Eve took that as an invitation and stepped off the stoop and crossed the yard.

"How's Grandma Gerty?" Katy asked, gently flicking a wet blue shirt.

"Still sleeping. I'm hoping the pain meds I picked up are helping."

"I heard about what happened in Buffalo." Katy's lips thinned and she seemed to take in the bruise on Eve's face. "I am thankful *Gott* was watching over you and Grandma Gerty."

The notion made Eve pause momentarily. Eve's crisis of faith might have compelled her to disagree, but Katy wasn't wrong. "We were very fortunate."

"Any news from the doctor?" Katy spun one way then the other to get a quick check on each of the babies.

"No, Mem needs more tests. But after the incident in the parking garage, I'm not convinced I'll get her to go again."

Katy made a tsking noise and Eve wasn't sure if it was in response to her or the children. "*Aii*, my goodness," her sister-in-law continued. "I tried to encourage Thomas to take her to another doctor, but he said we had to respect her wishes." Guilt and sadness softened her words.

Eve touched Katy's hand. "*Denki* for being there for my mother. I know she loves you." If things had turned out differently, the two women would have been close. Raising children together. Sharing gossip. A hollowness expanded in her belly. How was it possible to feel nostalgic for something she never had? For something she never wanted in the first place?

Back home, her closest friend was Suze. Her college roommate had been a lifesaver, welcoming her into her life. Introducing her to her mother. Providing her with a wonderful mentor and a sense of family that she no longer had. But there always seemed to be a disconnect between them. Eve assumed it was because she was hiding the biggest part of herself—her Amish past. Instead she told Suze half-truths about growing up out in farm country and being estranged from her family. Neither were untrue, but neither captured the whole story.

Far from it.

"The twins are getting so big." Eve knelt down on the grass and ignored the dew soaking into her sweatpants. Gracie toddled over and gently patted her aunt's face with curious determination. Perhaps she was noticing the dark spot under her eye. The little girl reached out and grabbed a fistful of her hair and tugged. Eve took her niece's sweet hand and pulled it away.

"She's always fascinated by my long hair when I comb it out," Katy said absentmindedly, then swiftly changed topics. "I've been wondering if Grandma Gerty is getting enough to eat. What do you think?" There was an eagerness in her questions, as if they had been running through her head for a long time.

"She could definitely eat more, but she insists she's not hungry." Eve had to be honest.

"I try to bring her a plate, but Thomas says we shouldn't cater to her. That it would make her lazy."

Eve could imagine her brother "putting my foot down," as he liked to say, especially to a teenaged Eve. "He has a strong personality." Eve chose her words carefully. "He was my big brother before he was your husband."

"You could have warned me," Katy deadpanned and they both burst out laughing. Obviously, Eve was just a child when her oldest brother married Katy. Her sister-in-law hid her smile behind a wet shirt she was about to hang on the line. She sniffed and took a beat to compose herself and said, "Thomas is a good man, and does what's best for our family."

"I know he loves you all," Eve said. "He respects the Amish way. I understand. And I love Grandma Gerty. But I'm not willing to leave things to chance. I need to make sure she gets the best possible care."

"She's afraid," Katy whispered. "You saw what your aunt went through when she had chemotherapy. It's not always a happy ending."

Eve's stomach twisted and she bit her lip. "Do you think I'm making a mistake?" She hated to voice her worry.

"You're still gathering information." Katy gave her a genuine smile. "See what the doctor says and go from there."

Eve nodded and fought the urge to pull her into a tight embrace. She truly appreciated her sister-in-law's support.

"What can I do?" Katy asked, then to Gabriel, "Oh, honey, give that to me." She reached down and unwrapped her son's chubby fingers from around a wooden clothespin that he had snagged and lifted to his lips. Gabriel's face crumbled and he threatened to let out a loud wail.

Eve held out her free arm and, to her surprise, her nephew ran to her and buried his sad face in her shoulder. She looked up at Katy and smiled, a bittersweet smile. She was going to miss these little ones.

"You have wonderful children," Eve said. "You must be proud."

A soft pink colored Katy's cheeks. "I am not proud."

"I didn't mean…" Eve rolled her eyes and laughed and she could see that Katy had a twinkle in her eye.

"I am very blessed." She paused a beat. "I wish there wasn't so much turmoil between you and Thomas."

"I'm afraid that will always be the case unless I was to come back and be baptized."

Eve's heart sank at Katy's hopeful expression. "Is there a chance? Even a glimmer?"

Eve glanced across the way. Her brother and his older sons had emerged from the barn and were headed toward the fields. She planted a soft kiss on Gabriel's forehead. He smelled so good. Then she looked up at Katy and shook her head. "I have a life in Buffalo."

Katy nodded curtly, her chin trembling. She held up a hand as if to say *give me a minute* before asking, "How does Mercy seem to you?"

"Fine, fine," she said quickly, not wanting to betray her niece's confidence. "Are you worried about something?"

"Thomas said she reminds him of you at that age."

Eve scratched her forehead to hide the grimace. "Yikes, I'll have to apologize to her."

"Oh no, no." Katy suddenly seemed contrite. "I didn't mean—All fathers want the best for their daughters."

Eve smiled tightly. "If there's something you're worried about, you can talk to me. I'm pretty good at keeping a secret."

Katy bent and grabbed the wicker handles of the laundry basket and straightened. "A mother wants that for her daughter, too. I want her to be a *gut* daughter and someday a *gut* wife and mother."

Eve felt compelled to ask her if that was really all she wanted for her daughter, but she stuffed down the question when she saw the love shining in her eyes. All Amish mothers wanted their children to be baptized and to marry a nice Amish partner.

"Grandma Gerty still hasn't given up hope of my finding a nice Amish boy. I hate to break her heart."

Katy smiled. "Have you told her about Deputy Kimble?"

Eve's gaze snapped to her sister-in-law's.

"Mr. Yoder stopped by earlier."

Eve's stomach bottomed out and the tranquility of the peaceful morning was shattered. "Must have been very early," Eve muttered, remembering the Amish gentleman passing her and Dylan on Main Street last night. "I thought you didn't listen to the gossip in town." She forced a casualness she didn't feel. It took her right back to seven years ago.

"I try, I try." Katy rested the laundry basket on one hip and stretched out her free hand to her daughter. "Can you bring Gab?"

"Of course." Eve gently tousled the little boy's hair. "Want a piggyback ride?"

The toddler scooted around to her back and grabbed her neck. She reached behind her to support his bottom and pushed to her feet and groaned. "I'm out of shape."

Katy glanced over her shoulder. Grace held her mother's hand and twisted and turned to watch her brother. "Momma, Momma!"

"Don't worry, Grace, I can give you a ride next," Eve offered as Katy paused at the door, holding it for Eve and her rider. The house wasn't air-conditioned, but the temperature was much cooler out of the bright sun. "Well, I'll—"

"Stay," Katy said. "Have you had breakfast?" Before she had a chance to answer there was a commotion at the back door. First twelve-year-old Abraham, followed by his little brother Jebediah. "Wash your hands, boys, then tell your sisters to come in to eat." The smell of fresh-baked muffins lingered in the air.

As Thomas brushed past his sister, he gave her a once-over. "Eve, you said you'd dress plain while you're here." The simple statement held a heavy accusation.

On reflex, Eve glanced down at her sweatpants with dark spots on her knees from when she had been playing with his children. "You're right. I did." She helped Gabriel slide off her back. Then to her sister-in-law she said, "Thank you for the invitation. I need to check on Grandma Gerty."

Katy handed her a plate with muffins covered with a clean dish towel, as if anticipating her departure. "They're fresh. If I remember correctly, you always enjoyed my blueberry muffins."

"*Denki*," Eve said, a little louder than she needed to, strictly for her brother's benefit. Then she met her beautiful sister-in-law's sad eyes. "Grandma Gerty and I enjoy all your cooking and baking. You've been very good to both of us. And it makes me feel better about…everything."

Eve could feel her brother's eyes boring into the back of her head as she slipped out of her childhood home. Now her brother's. A place she feared she'd never feel truly welcomed again.

CHAPTER 19

"You did great, little man!" Dylan held his hand out to his side for his four-year-old nephew Mason to give him a high five.

"Did you see me score?" he asked excitedly.

"Of course. We all saw it." Dylan glanced over at his former sister-in-law, Benji, and Eve who had been kind enough to accept his nephew's excited invitation to attend his soccer game.

"Is Eve going to come to our house for a cookout?" Without waiting for an answer, Mason plowed on. "Uncle Dylan fixed the grill and he said we could have hot dogs after the game if it didn't rain." He scrunched up his face and squinted at the sun. "I don't think it's going to rain."

Dylan placed his hand gently on his nephew's sweaty head. "I don't think it'll rain either."

"Come on, let's go!" Mason grabbed Eve's wrist and tugged her toward the parking lot. She glanced over her shoulder and mimed her uncertainty.

"Mason, my man, that's not how you ask a lady on a date."

Mason stopped in his tracks and rubbed his nose roughly,

as if he had an itch. Then he looked up at Eve. "You wanna have a hot dog? Uncle Dylan knows how to make them light so they don't have all those gross black marks on them."

"Mason, stop being so pushy," his mother scolded. "Eve, you're very welcome to come back to the house for a cookout if you'd like." Tessa held up her hand. "But no pressure, despite my son's insistence."

"Um..." Eve raised her eyebrows, as if she didn't know what to do, and her eyes locked with Dylan's.

Dylan threw in his two cents. "It would be awesome if you could join us." He felt a little bad—just a little—that Eve had gotten roped into his nephew's soccer game. He had been FaceTiming her this morning on the front porch when his nephew came strolling out. When she asked him what he was up to, he turned the question into an invitation which she graciously accepted. When she arrived at the fields, Dylan was thrilled to see her after a few day's absence. She had been backpedaling about their relationship ever since the night of their kiss. She kept telling him that her life was in Buffalo, and her career kept her too busy for a long-distance relationship, and her priority was her mom. The excuses were endless.

And valid.

A part of him worried that maybe the feelings were a bit lopsided, not that he'd share that with her. His last serious relationship had disintegrated when he pivoted from being a future law school graduate to settling for being a sheriff's deputy. All because he refused to leave his brother's kids. He didn't want to suffer that type of devastating one-two blow again, yet he couldn't continue to live with more what-ifs.

"I can drive over, if that's okay." Eve was talking to Tessa.

"Great. You know the house, right?" Tessa hesitated as if reconsidering. "Why doesn't Dylan drive over with you? I'll take the boys home."

Eve took a step backward and waved her off. "No, no, he'll give you a hand. I'll meet you there." Her eyes widened. "Generally I'd offer to make something, but since it's so last-minute, can I pick up a dessert from the bakery?"

"We're covered," Tessa said, seemingly amused with the situation for some reason.

"Great, great." The odd lilt in Eve's voice suggested she was uncomfortable. "I'll follow you guys."

They climbed into their respective vehicles, and out of habit Dylan slid behind the wheel of Tessa's car. In the back seat he overheard Benji telling his big brother that he liked Mommy's friend, to which Mason said in an exasperated tone, "She's Uncle Dylan's friend!"

"Uh-uh," Benji replied. "She's a girl. She's Mommy's friend."

Tessa shifted in her seat. "Why don't we call it a tie. Eve is Mommy's new friend thanks to Uncle Dylan."

In the rearview mirror, Mason jutted out his lower lip, obviously frustrated that his mother had played Switzerland. Eve pulled in behind them on the quiet road.

"So," Tessa said, turning her attention to him, "what is going on between you two?"

"Like my man said, we're friends." Dylan hated his forced, false tone.

"Nothing more?" Tessa spoke softly, nearly drowned out by his nephews' chatter.

"She's going back to Buffalo."

Tessa tugged on her seat belt to loosen it a bit. "That doesn't answer the question, but okay…" She let him off the hook fairly easily.

Dylan sighed. "Eve's great. We had fun the other night. But she has so much going on with her career and her mom's illness. I don't want to complicate things for her."

"Sounds like an excuse."

Dylan made an indecipherable sound.

"She's not Maggie," Tessa stated matter-of-factly.

He bristled at the mention of his college sweetheart. He met her shortly after Eve left Hunters Ridge. He had thought they'd be together forever until he realized she'd rather be married to a successful lawyer than a small-town sheriff's deputy. After shaking off the jolt her name had caused, he said, "No, she's not." Definitely not Maggie.

"Okay, I'll stop meddling."

Dylan scoffed. "You said that last time we chatted about Eve."

Tessa playfully threw up her hands. "And I'll probably remind you again in the future when it comes up."

He was about to protest, to tell his sister-in-law that he hadn't been the one to disappear without so much as a goodbye. No, protesting would blow his casual cover. He glanced up in the rearview mirror to see Eve's car behind them and something deep down in his gut ached. No, he didn't need to add fuel to the smoldering fire.

~

Eve didn't want the evening to end. She hadn't felt this relaxed in someone else's presence in a long time.

Her gaze slid to the large bird clock on the wall. It was close to ten. "Oh my." She pushed back from the kitchen table where she, Dylan, and Tessa had been chatting and sharing a bottle of wine. Mason and Benji had been running in and out of the room between watching cartoons. Their appearances had grown farther apart and Eve suspected it was because the last time they came in, their mother suggested it was their bedtime. Smart little boys that they were, they realized if they stayed out of sight, their mother might forget they were still up. However, Eve's announcement that she was leaving sent Tessa calling to the boys to go up and brush their teeth and get ready for bed.

"I didn't mean to stay so late," Eve said, suddenly feeling self-conscious.

"No, no..." Dylan said.

"Can Uncle Dylan read us a bedtime story?" Benji asked, his hair mussed from lying on the couch.

Tessa looked like she was about to tell her son no when Dylan pushed back from the table. "Of course, little man." As he passed Eve, he placed his hand on her shoulder. "Don't leave before I come back down."

"Oh, okay. I'll help Tessa clean up."

"No, you won't." Tessa smiled and grabbed the empty wineglasses and placed them in the sink and announced with a smile, "Done!" She returned to the table and sat down. "I enjoyed getting to know you tonight."

Eve was in awe of Tessa's easygoing spirit, especially after suffering such a devastating tragedy. It was like she consciously chose to be happy. "Thank you. I enjoyed getting to know you, too." Eve folded the paper napkin on the table in front of her, repeatedly dragging her index finger along the edge to sharpen the crease. "Dylan loves those boys." A strange feeling bubbled up inside her at the realization—not for the first time—that Dylan would make a wonderful father.

"I don't know what I'd do without him. He's been a godsend after Jacob died." Tessa's voice grew soft at the mention of her deceased husband.

The young mother's grief swept into the room and weighed heavily on Eve's chest. "I'm so sorry for your loss."

Tessa nodded her head slowly. "Sometimes it feels like a bad dream." She shrugged. "I knew Jacob was struggling, but I thought he was getting better." She pressed her lips together and waved her hand, as if dismissing the topic of conversation. "I'm so grateful for Dylan. And I've learned to make the best of it. My faith has helped."

Suddenly feeling uncomfortable, Eve pushed back and stood. "I should go." She swayed and grabbed the table to steady herself. "Whoa, the wine went right to my head." Embarrassment heated her face. "I usually don't drink that much. I'm a lightweight."

Tessa put her hand over Eve's. "Dylan can drive you home."

"My car..."

Her host smiled and gave her a knowing look. "Your car will be perfectly fine here."

"I suppose you're right." She picked up the empty bowl of chips and put it in the sink next to the wineglasses.

Just then Dylan came downstairs and something flashed in his eyes—surprise, perhaps, that she was still here. "I thought maybe you'd left."

Tessa gently touched Eve's elbow, as if to steady her. "I'm afraid our guest has had too much to drink."

"Are you okay to drive me home?" Eve asked. Heat tinged her skin and she wrote it off as the wine.

"Of course. I only had a little wine and that was hours ago."

Eve pressed a hand to her chest. "Oh wow, maybe I drank more than I thought." She giggled and pointed to Tessa. "Did we polish off that bottle?"

Tessa raised her eyebrows but didn't say anything.

Dylan slid his hand around Eve's back. "Come on, I'll get you home."

Eve was mostly quiet on the drive. When they arrived at the farm, she unbuckled and turned to face him. "Thanks."

"Of course." Something in his serious gaze kept her frozen in her seat. Dylan reached out slowly and cupped her cheek in his hand and planted a chaste kiss on her forehead.

Eve groaned and reluctantly pulled away. "You're making this all too hard."

He searched her face. "You've had a bit too much to drink. Let me see you to the door."

"You don't—" The determined look in his eyes made her stop midsentence. She should probably accept his offer. She didn't want to face-plant on the ground.

Dylan met her around the front of the truck and he gently took her elbow. "You okay?"

"I'm fine." She lifted her hand with her index finger and thumb an inch apart. "Might have a wee headache tomorrow, that's all."

Dylan reached up and caught her hand, then playfully threaded his fingers with hers. Electricity raced up her arm. She smiled and a breeze whispered across her warm skin.

The clouds swept across the night sky revealing the bright moon. As they approached the dawdy haus a dark shadow caught her attention. "What is that?" She dropped Dylan's hand and moved closer and teetered. She was dizzy. And the surge of adrenaline making her heart race didn't help.

Dylan planted his hands on each side of her waist to steady her. Tucking her safely under his arm, he grabbed his cell phone out of his pocket and aimed the flashlight app on the small stoop.

A pig had been violently slaughtered. Eve bit back a yelp and pressed her hand to her nose against the vile, rotting smell tinged with iron. "What in the world?"

Dylan lifted the beam of light. Splashed across the door in pig's blood was the single word: *SINNER.*

CHAPTER 20

*A*nger pulsed in Dylan's veins. Hyperaware of their surroundings, he tapped off the flashlight app. He struggled to focus on the dark landscape and his skin itched, as if someone was out there, watching them. He placed his hand on Eve's lower back. "Let's get you inside."

"No." The single word came out confident and strong. The moonlight reflected in the whites of her eyes, but he couldn't make out her features clearly. Somewhere in the black night a dog was barking, making him wary since even the animals sensed something was off.

"We need to call this in. Come on."

She shook her head slowly. "No, no, we can't. We've got to clean this up before Thomas sees it."

"What? Someone leaves a menacing threat on your doorstep and you want to cover it up and forget it happened?" He swiped his finger across the screen on his phone. "I'm calling it in."

"No, no, please. It's only going to cause more problems. My brother will make me leave." She pointed animatedly at the pig. "I know who did this."

"Brenneman," he said.

Eve searched his face, as if she was afraid to confide in him. Afraid of what he'd do. "Yes." There was a reluctance in that single word. "Don't you see? If I make a big deal of this, it'll cause more problems for me. There's nothing more Aaron'd like than for me to draw attention to myself, my family." Her voice broke. "I need this to go away." She glanced around. "And you have to help me."

Dylan caught her hands. "This isn't right. If Aaron did this, he must be held accountable."

Eve pinned him with a determined gaze. "We both know that's not how it works. I'll be the only one punished. Thomas won't like the attention and he'll ask me to leave. And I can't abandon my mom. Without me, she won't get the proper treatment."

Dylan sighed, frustration pulsing in his jaw. "Okay." He'd do anything for Eve. "I have a tarp in the back of my trunk. I can dispose of the pig. You'll need a bucket of water to scrub the graffiti off the door and the blood off the porch."

The moonlight caught a sad smile tugging on the corners of her mouth. "Thank you," she whispered. Something silent passed between them in the dark night that he couldn't quite hold on to. She cleared her throat and said, "Can you move your truck and turn on your headlights? I want to make sure we don't leave anything behind."

With a plan in place, Eve cautiously stepped over the slaughtered pig. Dylan moved his truck into position, then got out and opened the back hatch and slid out a few tarps he had picked up for his planned paint job. Unfortunately for Mason, it kept getting postponed for one reason or another. With tarps in hand, he turned and came up short. Thomas Reist blocked his path. He recognized him from town.

"What's going on?" he asked with an unmistakable Pennsylvania Dutch lilt. He was squinting in the direction of the small house. His chin jutted out, as if by drawing his head closer, he'd make sense of what he was seeing. His hair was mussed, as if he had been sleeping.

Dylan found himself momentarily speechless. He glanced toward Eve's mother's house and the disgusting mess. The door yawned open. Eve had slipped inside to get cleaning supplies. The graffiti wasn't visible from this vantage point, but the butchered animal was in full view. "Have you seen anyone on your property tonight?" Dylan asked.

"Besides you?" Thomas's eyes narrowed. "What is that?

Realizing he didn't have a choice, Dylan said, "Some someone dumped a pig on your mother's doorstep."

Dragging his hand repeatedly down his beard, Thomas stormed toward the crime scene. He reached the porch at the same time that Eve appeared with cleaning supplies. The metal bucket clacked on the porch and water whooshed over the sides.

"What's this?" Thomas demanded.

Eve's gaze floated to her brother, then Dylan, then back to her brother. He wanted to jump in and defend her, but something held him back. He suspected his defense of Eve would only make matters worse. "Seems the bishop's favorite grandson is at it again," she said drolly.

"What's that on the door?" Thomas asked, his voice held an accusatory tone.

Eve reached behind her and pulled the door closed. The blood dripped from the letters. "I'm removing it now. *Mem* will never see it."

Thomas shook his head. "Don't you understand? As long as you're here, this will continue."

"It's my fault?" Eve whispered in a strained voice.

Dylan spoke up. "You're the victim."

"This is a family matter," Thomas spit out.

Rage burned Dylan's gut. "Someone has to address this. Aaron Brenneman has been left unchecked for too long."

"Aaron is a jerk, but he's also the bishop's grandson. He can stir up a lot of trouble for us." Thomas's tone seemed to soften, as if it was getting too hard to continue to defend the indefensible.

Eve stood frozen watching her brother, as if she sensed what was coming next.

"You have to leave," Thomas said, apparently unable to side with his own sister over the grandson of the bishop.

Dylan bit back the harsh comment that sat on his tongue. Family should always come first. Always.

∽

The iron-rich air and her brother's demand made Eve want to retch. Or maybe it was all the wine she had consumed. She purposely took shallow breaths. "But *Mem*..." She took a step forward and almost tripped on the bucket.

"Have you been drinking?" Thomas's accusation brought her right back to her teenage years.

She squared her shoulders, forcing the reality of the situation to sober her up. "I am not leaving until I make sure *Mem* gets any necessary treatment."

Thomas held his hand up as if to silence her. His unkempt hair and beard formed a halo around his head in the truck's headlights. She could only imagine the expression on his face. "How do you think this kind of stress is going to be for her health? Not *gut*." He answered his own question. "You're selfish. You've always been selfish."

Her brother's harsh words heated her cheeks. Anger and embarrassment twisted her stomach into knots and made it impossible to think clearly. Why did her brother have to let loose in front of Dylan?

"Take it easy." Dylan spoke up, his voice gruff. "Your sister had nothing to do with this."

Eve's blood chugged through her veins and despite appreciating having someone in her corner, she wanted him to be quiet. An outsider would never convince her devout Amish brother that he was in the wrong.

As Eve feared, Thomas spun to face off with Dylan. "You haven't helped this situation one bit. You were a negative influence on my sister when she was a teenager, and now you're making her the subject of gossip. Again."

"Your sister is a strong woman. She has her own mind." Dylan continued to defend her.

Eve fisted her hands. And waited. It didn't take long.

"No one ever denied that. What's she's lacking is honesty."

Eve pressed her hand to her chest, feeling like she had been stabbed and her brother was twisting the knife. She might not have always made the right decisions—she was human, after all—but she always acted with integrity. "You're not being fair, Thomas. Let's talk about this tomorrow when we've had time to calm down."

"I'm not going to change my mind. You promised Mem you'd act and dress as one with this community, and you've gone against that from the beginning."

"No one expected me to wear plain clothing to run errands. Driving a car in a long dress would have been a mockery."

"You didn't even try," her brother spit out. "If you could have maintained a low profile, that would have been one thing. But to get news of your indiscretion with this outsider on Main Street is further embarrassment to our family."

Eve's nerves buzzed. Why couldn't Mr. Yoder have kept his mouth shut?

Before Eve had a chance to protest, Thomas said, "I want

you out by morning. I'll take care of Mother like I've always done."

Eve pressed her lips together and didn't say anything for fear she'd break into tears. She watched in shocked silence as her brother stormed back into his home across the lane.

"I'm sorry," Dylan said.

Eve closed her eyes and a tear slid down her cheek. After taking a moment to compose herself, she found her voice. "Please get the tarp and wrap this poor thing up."

"Of course."

Dylan and Eve worked in silence as they cleaned up the slaughtered pig. He tossed the cumbersome package in the back of his truck. "I'll make sure I dispose of this properly."

"Thank you." She peeled off rubber gloves and tossed them on the porch.

"Eve..."

She pressed her hand on his chest and went up on her tiptoes to kiss his cheek. "I don't want to discuss it."

"Okay," he said, seemingly resigned.

She turned to go inside, then spun back around. "My car is at Tessa's. I'm going to need it."

"I'll pick you up in the morning. What time?"

Eve needed time to break the news to her mother. Maybe talk some sense into Thomas. "How about eleven?"

"See you then." He took a step backward. "Sleep well. Things will work out."

She nodded even though she didn't agree. Not in the least. She had been home less than a week and everything had gone to pot. Any hopes of a reconciliation with her family were gutted like that poor pig.

CHAPTER 21

"Thanks for taking a ride with me," Dylan said to Caitlin as he sat shotgun in her patrol car the next morning. His fellow deputy was on duty, whereas he had the day off. He wanted to roll up to the Brenneman house in a pseudo-official capacity.

Dylan had done a little digging. He learned Aaron worked at the cheese factory in Hunters Ridge. If he confronted the man's wife alone, she might unwittingly offer some information on her husband's whereabouts last night. And he hoped Mrs. Brenneman would be more likely to talk to Caitlin.

"No problem." Caitlin dipped her head and stared out the window as the farms rolled past. "You know, the Grabers run a hog farm next door to the Brennemans. Maybe we should talk to them, too. See if one of their hogs is missing. Or maybe Aaron flat out bought one from them."

"Wouldn't that be convenient?" Dylan deadpanned.

Elmer Graber had come on the sheriff's department's radar after he harassed one of Hunters Ridge's more prominent residents in retribution for his sister's tragic murder in

New York City. Turns out, Eve hadn't been the first, nor would she be the last Amish person to leave the community.

"Aaron could still explain it away," Caitlin said. "Claim he bought it for the meat."

"Let's see what the wife has to say." Dylan studied the tranquil farm, wondering what actually went on behind closed doors. He tapped on the passenger window. "Pull into their lane."

"You think that's a good idea? You're looking to fan the flames, aren't you?" Even as Caitlin questioned his judgment, she did as he requested. The patrol car bobbled over the deep ruts sliced into the earth from the narrow buggy wheels.

"Maybe our presence will give Lena Brenneman a little motivation to hurry up and talk to us so that we get off her property. You know how cruel small-town gossips can be."

Caitlin slanted him a look. No doubt she detected the hard edge to his tone. "This is personal, isn't it?"

Dylan eyed his coworker. Caitlin Flagler didn't miss much. That was what made her a solid deputy. "We're not supposed to make things personal."

She smirked. "Yeah, I hear ya."

That was what he liked about working with her—she knew when to let things go. And he knew better than to tell her that he was annoyed that the darn rumor mill in Hunters Ridge was about to chase Eve Reist away. Again. If he could do something to punish the jerk who thought it was appropriate to threaten her, then he'd have some measure of satisfaction. And maybe, just maybe, she'd stay. At least for the rest of her vacation as she had planned. And, selfishly, he wanted a chance to get to know her more. Dismissing his wandering thoughts, he glanced at the clock on the cruiser's dash. He had promised to pick Eve up at eleven since she had left her car at Tessa's place last night. They needed to speed this up. "You ready?"

"Always."

They both climbed out and headed toward the door. The farm was smaller than most—a small vegetable garden and a greenhouse. There was a wooden stand out front which suggested they sold some of their produce, most likely to tourists. Their primary income came from Aaron's job at the factory. More and more Amish had to count on outside jobs as land got more precious.

An Amish woman he suspected was Lena Brenneman opened the door before they reached the porch steps. She had a small child on her hip and another one stood and played shyly in the folds of her long dress. The look of concern in the woman's eyes suggested she feared something had happened to her husband.

"Hello?" The quiet greeting sounded more like a question.

"Is your husband here, ma'am?" Caitlin asked, as she and Dylan had rehearsed.

He was already feeling a bit like a heel for bothering the woman. If her husband was threatening Eve, it wasn't her fault. When she discovered he had been harassing a former girlfriend, the pain and humiliation would be doubled.

"Um, no, he works at the factory in town." She lifted her downcast gaze and if he hadn't been studying her carefully, he might have missed the flash of anger in her eyes before she looked away again. She took a step backward and reached blindly for the doorknob behind her. "You'll have to come back later if you want to talk to him."

"Actually," Dylan said, "we'd like to talk to you."

One of her brows drew down. She seemed to clutch the child in her arms tighter and she reached with her fingers to touch the other child's head.

"Perhaps we should go inside," Caitlin suggested. She glanced over her shoulder toward the road, as if to say, *So the neighbors won't talk.* She was good at her job.

"Oh, I don't know." The Amish woman's gaze traveled behind them to the patrol car sitting squarely in the driveway. The neighbors would be chatting about this visit either way.

"We'd rather not talk in front of the children," Dylan said.

"What is this about? I have a lot of work to do and don't have time to be standing here on the porch." Surprisingly, a hard edge of steel laced her tone. Perhaps she had been anticipating a visit from the sheriff's department.

"Do you know Eve Reist?" Dylan asked.

The color drained from Lena's face and she swayed back a bit.

Caitlin held out her arms for the child. "Perhaps you want to sit down."

Instead of going inside, Lena sidestepped to the rocking chair on the porch and slowly lowered herself into it. She settled one child in her lap. Her other daughter tucked herself behind the chair and watched them with curiosity. "*Yah*, I know who she is." She looked up with pity in her eyes. "I hear poor Mrs. Reist is sick."

"Yes, she is. That's why what happened last night is especially troubling."

Pink infused Lena's cheeks. "What happened?" Was she surprised? Or had she been dreading this moment? Dylan was having a hard time deciding. One minute she was angry, the next deeply concerned.

"I was hoping you could tell us, Mrs. Brenneman," Caitlin said. "Have you heard any gossip?"

The young mother adjusted the fabric of the dress of the child in her lap. "With their mouths the godless destroy their neighbors, but through knowledge the righteous escape."

Caitlin must have noticed the muscle ticking in Dylan's jaw because she gently touched his arm and said, "You're a God-fearing woman, Lena, but we're worried for Eve's safety. Do you know anything about the slaughtered pig left on her doorstep last night?" She got right to the point, hating that the child had to hear this.

Lena lifted her gaze. "A pig?" Her voice cracked. "Why would someone do that?"

"Apparently they think she's less than God-fearing," Caitlin said. She omitted the part about the word *SINNER* written on the door in blood.

Dylan carefully studied the nonverbal cues the woman was giving off. She seemed to be trembling. "Mrs. Brenneman, do you know anything about that?"

The child behind the chair looked up with keen interest. "Elmer feeds pigs." Her face twisted up in disgust. "It stinks." The child had a subtle lisp.

"Elmer?" Dylan asked, wanting to hear it directly from the little girl.

Lena shot her daughter a cautionary gaze that she ignored. The child lifted her finger. "He lives there." She pointed toward the house across the field. "He let me pet one once. His nose was slimy."

"That must have been fun," Caitlin said. "Did the pig have a name?" His partner was very good at bonding with the children.

"No, silly," she said. "You don't name them! You eat them."

Caitlin slanted Dylan a look and they both flashed smiles, then quickly schooled their expressions. No truer words.

"Mrs. Brenneman," Dylan asked, "did your husband recently purchase a pig? Or perhaps Elmer gave him one."

Lena let out a huge huff. "Stand up," she said as she removed her younger daughter from her lap and planted her on her feet. Lena rose, swatted at the folds of her skirt and marched toward the door. She held out her hand for her other daughter. Before Lena went in, she said, "I have no idea what you're talking about. You need to leave."

"Mrs. Brenneman..." Dylan glanced down at the little faces of her daughters watching him with anticipation. He selected his words carefully. "We can help you and your daughters..." If Aaron Brenneman was the kind of man to chase Eve after she refused his advances and saw fit to leave a slaughtered pig on her porch, there was no telling what he might be doing to his wife behind closed doors.

Lena slowly shook her head and ushered her daughters inside. She paused in the doorway. "My family does not need your interference." She closed the door with a solid click.

As Dylan and Caitlin headed back to the cruiser, he said, "I don't think it's a coincidence that the Grabers next door have a pig farm."

"I'll drop you at the station so you can grab your vehicle. I know you have to pick up Eve at eleven." Caitlin talked to him over the top of the cruiser. "Then I'll check on our friend Elmer. He's up to something."

"That would be fantastic." He glanced across the field, the barn of the neighboring property visible between the trees. He wanted to go himself, but he had full confidence in Caitlin to assess the situation without him.

CHAPTER 22

Over breakfast, Eve explained to Grandma Gerty that she'd be headed back to Buffalo. She claimed that she had some work-related things she had to get done, and that she'd be able to return to Hunters Ridge to take her mother to her medical appointments—that is, if she would agree to go. Eve resented her brother's demands that she leave, yet she couldn't ignore him. This was technically his home and she was merely a guest. And even if she pushed it, the tension and stress wouldn't be good for Mem. That much her brother was right on.

Using the surge of energy from the pure maple syrup generously doused on her mother's apple pancakes, Eve grabbed her suitcase out of the closet and tossed it on the bed. The quick motion made her brain hurt. She vowed to never overindulge in wine again. *Ugh.* As she emptied each drawer and dumped the contents into her suitcase, she felt the tears burning the back of her eyes. She had not wanted to leave on these terms.

She sensed before she saw her mother standing in the

doorway, leaning heavily on her cane. "This doesn't have to do with your work. Something happened..."

Not wanting to stir anything more up, yet not willing to lie, Eve said, "Please don't worry. It's probably better this way." She could only imagine how hard it was for Katy and Thomas to raise children in the Amish way. Most children did stay and follow the rules of the Amish, but if they did leave, it was devastating to the family.

"Please don't say that." Her mother slowly crossed the room and sat down heavily on the rocking chair and had to brace herself against the arm when it tilted back suddenly. "You said you'd try."

Eve stopped folding one of her T-shirts and lowered herself onto the edge of the bed. "Try?"

"I thought you were going to follow the *Ordnung*. That maybe you'd stay for *gut*."

Eve's heart sank. "I never planned on staying. I only agreed to dress plain out of respect for you." She placed the T-shirt in the suitcase and smoothed her hand across it. Eve hadn't even honored that small part of her promise. "I'm sorry I didn't try harder." She tilted her head. "I won't be staying here, but I'm not going to stay away." She couldn't. They had no idea what they were dealing with health-wise.

A quiet knock sounded on the exterior door.

"Who is that?" Grandma Gerty asked, pushing to her feet.

"It must be Dylan. He's picking me up. I left my car at his sister-in-law's last night." She quickly grabbed her cosmetics from the dresser and stuffed them into the suitcase and zipped it up.

"Does he make you happy?" Her mother's out-of-the-blue question startled her, making her stop and turn around.

"What?" Heat infused Eve's face.

"For a worldly woman, you sure don't know how to

bluff." A twinkle lit her mother's eyes. "If you're going to walk away from your family again, I pray it's for a man who deserves you."

A sliver of indignation raced up her spine. "I left for me. Not a man."

Her mother paused and stared at her. "Then let me rephrase that. If you're not going to find a nice Amish man, I hope you find a nice, decent man."

Eve shrugged, not sure what to say.

A knock sounded on the door again. "You better get that. Or should I?" Her mother took a small shuffle-step toward the door.

"I got it." Eve hoisted her tote on her shoulder and rolled the suitcase behind her.

She opened the door and Dylan gave her a once-over. "Are you leaving?" The disappointment in his tone made her heart flutter.

"We can talk in the truck."

"Okay." He reached out and took her suitcase from her. He angled his head and greeted her mother standing behind her. "How are you doing today, Mrs. Reist?"

"Fine, fine."

"I'll see you soon, okay Mem?" Eve leaned in and brushed a kiss across her cheek. The smell of her face lotion brought back a million memories of growing up as Gerty Reist's daughter. Eve would never be okay with being estranged from her family. And regardless of whatever tentative agreement she and her brother might reach, her visits to her childhood home would always be somewhat uncomfortable. That was simply the way it was.

"I'm fine here. Everything is fine," her mother said.

Eve swallowed around a knot of emotion in her throat, knowing that by walking out this door she'd have little chance of convincing her mother to pursue treatment—if it ended up being cancer—in Buffalo. Her mother was already afraid and recent events didn't make it easier. Eve paused on the porch for one last moment. "I love you."

"You're a *gut* girl," her mother said.

Eve fought back tears. It felt like a permanent goodbye.

Holding onto her composure by a thread, Eve rushed to Dylan's truck and hopped in, stuffing her bag at her feet. He placed her suitcase in back then slipped in behind the wheel. His compassionate gaze made her heart ache. He was going to be one more person she had to disappoint, and she wasn't sure how much more she could take.

Dylan cleared his throat. "Are you okay?"

All she could muster was a slow shake of the head.

"You couldn't convince Thomas to let you stay?"

She shook her head again.

Dylan reached over and touched her knee. "I'm sorry."

"Me, too," she squeaked out. Her gaze drifted to the *dawdy haus*, and she imagined Grandma Gerty inside making herself a cup of tea. All alone. She let out a long breath between tight lips. "Can we go?"

"Of course."

As Dylan maneuvered the truck out of the lane, Eve caught sight of Mercy sitting on the porch steps looking dejected. How had she missed her? "Hold up!"

Eve pulled on the door handle at the same time as Dylan came to a stop. She jogged over to her niece who frowned and asked, "Weren't you going to say goodbye?"

"I'll be back to take Grandma Gerty to her doctor's appointments."

Mercy gave a slight shake of her head. "No you won't." There was a bitterness to her tone.

"*Yah.* I will."

Mercy lifted her thin shoulders then let them drop.

The door behind Mercy opened and Thomas appeared. "I see you're headed out."

Eve nodded. "Make sure you call my cell if anything changes with Mother."

The subtle twitch of Thomas's lips suggested he would, even if he wouldn't outwardly agree to it.

"I'm sorry if I..." She hated that she had to apologize when she was the victim. She was about to take it back, when instead she said, "I'm sorry Aaron Brenneman is still a jerk. And I'm not going to let him stop me from taking care of Mother."

"Katy and I will make sure Grandma Gerty is well cared for." The soft tone of Thomas's voice was unfamiliar to her.

Eve's gaze swept from her brother's to her niece's. She took a step backward. "You have a beautiful family, Thomas. Thank you for allowing me to stay in your home." She flicked a wave and jogged back to the truck.

"All set?" Dylan asked.

"As I'll ever be..." she muttered.

~

Dylan pulled into Tessa's driveway. "Why don't you come in and say hello to the boys?"

Eve seemed hesitant, but she didn't have a choice when Mason and Benji bolted out of the door. "Where were you?" Benji asked Eve. "Your car's been here *all* day."

Eve's face flushed with embarrassment. Knowing it wasn't wise to tell a six-year-old that his new friend had too much to drink, Dylan spoke up first, "Miss Eve was tired, so I gave her a ride home last night."

"You're not tired now?" Mason asked.

Eve smiled. If the dark marks under her eyes were any

indication, she was very tired. "I'm not as tired as I was last night."

"Oh." His youngest nephew seemed to notice the suitcase Dylan had pulled out of his truck to transfer to her vehicle. "Are you going on a trip?"

"I'm headed home."

Mason's brow furrowed the way it did when he was figuring out a puzzle. "Where's home?"

"Buffalo."

His eyebrows shot up. "We go to the mall in Buffalo. And the zoo!" Then he grew concerned again. "But that's, like, a really long car ride. My mom makes us go pee before we get into the car."

Eve laughed. "That's always a good idea. But the drive isn't too bad," she thoughtfully reassured him.

Tessa came outside drying her hands on a dish towel. "Now I see why the boys were so excited." She tilted her head toward the house. "Come in for lunch."

"I…" Eve let the single word trail off. Indecision creased the fine lines under her eyes. Her bruise had taken on an angry purple hue that seemed to be muted by concealer.

"I didn't realize you were leaving Hunters Ridge already," Tessa said.

"Long story." Eve tucked a strand of hair behind her ear.

"It must be hard." Tessa said so much in those four little words.

An idea started to formulate in Dylan's head, but he didn't want to be presumptuous. "She hadn't planned on leaving. Her brother asked her to."

"Oh…" Tessa's surprised expression reminded Dylan of her sons. "How is your mother?"

"She's a tough one. I just hope she lets me take her to Buffalo for more tests."

Mason wrapped his arms around Dylan's waist and tried

to lift his legs. Dylan grunted at the weight of his nephew hanging off him like a monkey. He gently peeled off the boy's arms and set him firmly on the ground. "Go play on the jungle gym in back." He had spent a good chunk of a summer weekend putting together a massive play set from one of the local lumberyards. Without waiting to be asked again, the two boys bolted around to the back of the house.

Tessa dropped her arm and let the dish towel dangle by her side. "There's plenty of room here if you'd like to stay. I have a spare bedroom."

Dylan smiled to himself.

Eve's eyebrows drew up slightly. "I couldn't impose."

"Truly…" Tessa took a step forward and grabbed the handle of Eve's suitcase, as if she wasn't going to take no for an answer. "It would be my pleasure. And Benji and Mason would *love* to have you around." She stuck out her lower lip and blew the fine hairs away from her face. "Unless you'd rather not." She frowned. "Not sure how you feel about having two precocious little guys who are always"—she pointed in the direction they ran—"this full of energy."

A soft smile brightened Eve's face and some of the tension seemed to ease around her eyes. "Thank you. I would love to stay in Hunters Ridge, at least until I know my mother is all set."

Tessa dragged the towel through her hands. "Good, I'm glad it's settled."

"I'll bring her things in," Dylan offered.

The gravel crunched under Tessa's feet as she turned to walk away. "I better go check on the boys." She called over her shoulder, "There's fresh lunch meat and anything else you might want in the fridge."

"Thank you," Eve and Dylan said in unison.

Dylan placed his free hand on Eve's lower back, and he sensed the heaviness from earlier lifting. Hopefully, before she left for good, he could hold Aaron Brenneman responsible for harassing her, and the Buffalo police department could track down her attacker in the hospital parking garage.

For a woman who claimed to live a quiet life, Eve Reist sure attracted a lot of unwanted attention.

CHAPTER 23

During the afternoon, Eve and Dylan had taken the boys on a hike on the trail leading up the escarpment. Mason had reminded his uncle that they were supposed to paint his room, but he was easily swayed with the promise of a new adventure. The bright blue sky and refreshing soft breeze made it a perfect afternoon to be outside. She had forgotten how exhausting a hike could be, but she enjoyed every minute of it. She also got a kick out of the boys showing her every pine cone, tree branch and rock they found. "Look, Miss Eve. Look! Look!"

Eve was grateful for Tessa's hospitality, and she was also grateful for the extra time spent with Dylan. After dinner, they moved out onto the back patio while the boys settled in for some cartoons with their mother. Eve suspected Tessa would rather be outside enjoying the summer evening, but had begged off to give her and Dylan some time alone.

Eve took a long sip of her soft drink. "I think Tessa is conspiring to push us together."

Dylan lowered his beer bottle and smiled. "Do you think we need her help?"

Eve mirrored his smile and shook her head, taking another sip of her drink.

"Are you sure you don't want some wine?" Dylan asked.

"No, thank you." Eve traced a finger down the condensation on her glass. "I'm going to stick with soda for now." She rarely consumed too much alcohol, but when she did she always regretted it. Giving herself a headache was not her favorite thing to do.

"I'm sorry things didn't work out with your family," Dylan said, seemingly out of the blue.

"Yeah…" Eve let the single word drag on. "That wasn't much of a surprise. I imagine it was wishful thinking to believe I could come back home after seven years and patch things up, especially when memories are long, especially around here." Dylan had leaned forward, like he was about to tell her something, when she lifted her finger and said, "Hold that thought. I want to reach out to my brother before it gets too late. Let him know I'm still in town, in case…in case my mother needs anything. He has a phone tucked away in one of the small buildings on the property."

"The Amish tend to figure things out, don't they?" Dylan leaned back and took another long drink of his beer.

Eve shrugged, then found the number. She was surprised when Mercy answered, her voice soft and tentative.

"Hey Mercy, it's Eve." She rose to her feet and stepped away from Dylan, as if that might make her hear better.

"He made you leave, didn't he?" Mercy bit out the words. Her tone was filled with anger and disrespect.

Eve's stomach dropped. Their conversation earlier had been interrupted by Thomas. "Your father means well. He has a responsibility to you and your siblings. He's a *gut* man." Part of her felt like she was reading from a script. Another part wanted desperately to make sure Mercy didn't have a falling-out with her father. Being on the outside looking in was a lonely place to be.

"*Gut*? He made you leave." Her niece's voice cracked.

"Leaving Hunters Ridge was my choice. I wasn't going to stay much longer."

"You need to help Grandma Gerty. My *dat* won't do everything that needs to be done." The anger in Mercy's voice softened and gave way to something more heartbreaking. "I can't lose her, too."

A band of emotion compressed Eve's lungs, making it difficult to draw in a decent breath of air. Dylan was dutifully staring over the yard, as if he wasn't listening to every word. She wrapped her arm around her midsection. "I'm staying at Tessa Kimble's house in town. I plan to get Grandma Gerty the care she needs. Okay? I'm not abandoning her." *Or you.* But she couldn't say those words out loud. "Will you let your parents know?" Eve turned back around and smiled sadly at Dylan.

"Okay," Mercy said, seemingly resigned. "But I don't think my *dat* is going to want to see you."

Something in her tone set off alarm bells. "Did something else happen?"

"The bishop was here again. Your friend was over at the Brennemans' farm accusing Aaron of leaving the pig on Grandma Gerty's doorstep."

"What happened?" Her pulse quickened, and she narrowed her gaze at Dylan as she pressed the phone to her ear. He set his beer down on the table next to him and leaned forward and his features grew pinched.

"The bishop warned us that our family shouldn't welcome you in our home." Mercy's voice cracked. "He's tired of warning us."

Eve dug her fingers into the crown of her head. "I'm

sorry. I didn't know they were going to do that. Everything will be okay," she said reflexively.

"*Neh*, it won't," Mercy bit out.

"What does this mean for you and Roy?" Eve held her breath, fearing her actions had ruined Mercy's relationship with the young man.

"Don't worry about it." Teenage angst was universal.

"I'm here if you need anything, okay? I'll leave a message before I go back to Buffalo." Then thinking about the fact that Mercy had answered the phone, Eve said, "Were you expecting a call?"

Silence stretched across the line a beat before Mercy said, "*Neh, neh...*"

Eve detected a lie in her niece's response, but decided not to call her on it. In a world where everyone had a stake in what she did, Mercy needed some secrets. Eve had been eighteen once. She prayed that if her niece truly needed something, she'd reach out to her. "You have my cell phone number, right? Tell your mother and father I'm still in town. *Please.*"

"Okay." Then Mercy's voice grew quieter, as if she had moved the phone away from her mouth. "I have to go."

Eve tapped the screen, then set her phone on the table. "You went to the Brennemans. I asked you not to interfere." She dropped in the chair and leaned back.

"That type of behavior can escalate." He searched her face with his warm brown eyes, apparently seeking both understanding and forgiveness.

"I've handled my share of harassment in Buffalo. I can handle myself."

He reached out and touched her knee. "You don't have to. I'm here."

"I didn't ask you," she repeated, her anger growing. "You know how hard things are. I'll be lucky if my brother allows me on his farm." Eve stood and paced the small space. "I don't need anyone to do things for me. I can manage my own life."

Dylan reached out and caught her hand gently as she passed. "Please...I didn't..."

She squeezed his hand, wanting nothing more than to sit down next to him and rest her head on his chest. They locked gazes, but she couldn't bring herself to bridge the gap. She slid her hand out from his and crossed her arms over her chest. "I don't need you."

Dylan pushed to his feet with a heavy sigh. "Good night, Eve." He brushed past her on his way into the house.

Eve heard him say goodbye to his sister-in-law. She waited a bit until she couldn't handle the mosquitos biting at her legs and the loneliness of her thoughts, then she went inside. She found Tessa alone in the family room putting away the boys' toys. Eve decided to help, gathering the small plastic building blocks spread across the floor.

"You don't have to do that," Tessa said.

The tinkling of the plastic blocks grew louder. "I don't mind."

Tessa froze with a handful of action figures. "Everything okay with you and Dylan?"

Eve sat back on her heels and sighed. "Coming back to Hunters Ridge was a mistake."

"Why?"

"It reminded me of everything I ran away from."

Tessa tossed the toys into a bin, then turned around. "Would one of those things be Dylan?"

Eve felt a smile pulling at the corners of her mouth, but couldn't give voice to the obvious.

Tessa smiled in return. "I haven't seen him this happy since before...well, in a long time."

Dylan hadn't slept well, replaying everything he had said to Eve last night. He hadn't meant to crowd her—he knew how she felt about being told what to do—but he was worried about her. Worried what Aaron Brenneman might do if he continued to feel threatened by her. The man seemed to be unstable and his behavior was escalating.

Dylan decided today would be the day he'd finally paint his nephew's room. He swung by the hardware store and the elderly owner was working this morning. A young Amish man efficiently took his paint swatch and mixed up a gallon of navy paint. Tessa had convinced Mason to use two colors.

"That's a pretty bold color," the old man said, leaning heavily on the glass counter.

"My nephew has bold tastes. You have a better suggestion, Russ?"

"Hold on to your receipt?" The gentleman laughed. He'd worked here for as long as Dylan could remember. Only more recently had he gotten some extra help, mostly young Amish men looking to make a few extra bucks. "Well, we're here if he changes his mind."

Dylan laughed. "Thank you." He paid and headed out to his truck. He was glad he had an excuse to go over to Tessa's because he suspected Eve wasn't going to be happy to see him.

When he pulled up in Tessa's driveway, the reverse lights on Eve's car popped on, then immediately went off. Instead of moving, he climbed out of the truck and approached the driver's side of her car, surprised and disappointed to find her leaving. Eve hit the button and the window slid down. "Going somewhere?" he asked.

Eve rolled her eyes, but he detected a twinkle behind her feigned annoyance. "I need to face up to something I've been avoiding since I was all, 'I can manage my own life' last night."

Dylan planted his hand on the roof of her car and leaned in. "I'm sorry about interfering, especially when you asked me not to. It's the deputy in me. I didn't mean to cause more trouble with your family."

Eve angled her face up toward him. "You're not Amish. You can't have any idea what it's like. I needed to keep the peace long enough to convince my mother to pursue all her options for the treatment of her cancer." She quickly corrected herself. "If it's cancer."

"I'm sorry," he repeated. His overwhelming sense of right and wrong sometimes prevented him from seeing shades of gray. "Will you forgive me?"

Eve gripped the top of the steering wheel and laughed woefully. "I suppose I can forgive you. I did grow up Amish, after all."

He gently tapped the roof of the car with the side of his fist. "Where are you going?"

"Buffalo."

He rolled back on his heels and a wave of something he didn't want to explore washed over him. "You're leaving now?"

"Just a little road trip. I'll be back."

"Good." He studied her face. *Good!*

"Our conversation last night got me thinking."

"It did?"

"Yeah, but I have to get going now..." She shrugged, as if she was about to say goodbye, but instead she asked, "What brought you here this morning?"

"Promised the little man I'd paint his room." He gestured with his thumb toward his truck. "Can't put it off any longer."

Just then his nephews appeared on the porch with their

mother. Benji had a soccer ball tucked under his arm. "Hey, Uncle Dylan!"

"Hey there. I thought we were going to paint Mason's room."

"They did a last-minute reschedule of Benji's game." Tessa frowned. "Sorry."

"But Mom, I wanted to help paint," Mason whined.

"Any chance you could do it another time?" Tessa asked. "I want Mason to go to his brother's game."

Dylan took a step back and held up his palms. "Of course." It wouldn't take much to talk him out of painting.

"Looks like your day just freed up," Tessa said. "Maybe Eve could use some company."

Dylan looked at Eve and she smiled, an uncertain look on her face. "I'm sure Eve can manage on her own. She's an independent woman."

Eve laughed. He wasn't sure why. "Come to think of it. I wouldn't mind the company."

"Really?"

"Yes, really." She jerked her head toward the passenger seat. "Move your truck so we can get going before I change my mind."

"I have a better idea. I'll drive."

Eve shut off the engine and opened her door. Dylan stepped back a fraction and Eve climbed out.

They stood inches apart and he whispered. "I am sorry."

She patted his chest playfully. "Don't do it again."

They locked gazes for a long minute before Mason tapped his leg and he looked down. "Hey, what's up buddy?"

"Don't paint my room without me."

"I won't. I promise." His nephew was learning patience, that was for sure.

Eve slipped past him and opened the passenger side door

of his truck. "Maybe I can help paint, too. I'm good at cutting in around the windows."

Mason's eyes grew wide and he nodded. He ran over to his mom and said, "Miss Eve's helping paint my room."

Dylan's heart melted. They were all going to really miss Eve when she left Hunters Ridge for good.

CHAPTER 24

*D*ylan put his truck in park, and Eve followed his wide gaze to the mansion where her good friend Suze grew up. "Nice house," he muttered. "What does your mentor do for a living again?"

"You really don't watch TV, do you?"

"I told you…" He tilted his head and studied her with warm brown eyes. She couldn't stay mad at him even though his actions yesterday turned her burning embers of conflict with her family into a raging forest fire. "Carol Oliver is a legendary newscaster in Buffalo. She retired a few years ago, but still does the talk circuit and she has tremendous sway over the hiring and firing decisions at my station. Basically, she has a lot of connections."

"Okay, and you met her through your college friend Suze Oliver."

"Exactly." Eve rubbed her neck to ease out the kinks. "I couldn't reach Suze. She must have her phone on silent. Anyway, I need to get advice from Carol so I don't implode my career."

"The career you're not even sure you want."

Eve frowned. "Gotta pay the bills." She opened the truck door. "Meet me back here in an hour?"

"Sure thing. Tessa texted me a shopping list." The closest locations for some big department stores were in Buffalo. "If you need me sooner, text me."

Eve patted her small purse. "Got it. See you then." She paused as she climbed out of the truck. "Thanks for driving."

"Any time."

Eve slammed the door and walked up to the elaborate double doors of the home that screamed money. Family money. But Carol Oliver had climbed her way to the top in an era where local TV news was king. The melodic chime of the doorbell vibrated through the house followed by the staccato sound of high heels on the marble entryway. When perfectly coiffed Mrs. Oliver answered the door, her eyes widened and she grabbed Eve's bicep and pulled her in.

"Evelyn, what if someone saw you?"

Eve frowned. *Saw me?* She ran a hand down her long ponytail and suddenly felt very self-conscious. She hadn't bothered with make-up except for some concealer on her bruise, but based on her mentor's reaction, she realized it was a mistake.

"Your photo would be plastered all over that Tweeter or whatever." The older woman welcomed her inside and waved her hand, not caring what the various social media platforms were called, but she was fully aware of their power to make or break careers.

"Since when do you answer the door yourself?"

Carol laughed. "I'm not a monster. I give my employees the occasional day off."

Eve smiled tightly. "I saw the pool guy's truck in the driveway."

Carol waved her hand as if the answer was obvious. "The heat has made the pool a bear to keep clear. I don't want a green, stinky mess in the yard." Her diamond sparkled in the light. "That's not what you're here to talk about now, is it? Come."

Carol's heels clacked on the marble floor as they made their way to a cozy sitting room off the kitchen. A small tray of cheese and crackers and fancy sparkling water sat on the coffee table in front of a love seat.

"My Suze had a lot to tell me about you." The older woman pressed her hands together as she settled in next to Eve. "You're going to go far in this industry."

Eve tilted her head. "How so?"

"If you can keep your past buried that deep, you've got this figured out." She made a tsking noise. "You kept growing up Amish a secret. Amazing." Carol tapped her fingers together. "However, now that Suze knows, it may leak out. And I heard your mother was with you when one of those overzealous fans approached you in the parking garage." Eve was about to ask her how she knew when she mouthed, *Suze*.

She cleared her throat. "That's why I stopped by. How did you like being in the spotlight for all those years? I'm not sure it's for me."

"Oh, Suze told me you were having second thoughts about the big job."

"I didn't…" Eve didn't know what she thought.

Carol held up her palms, indicating her gorgeous home. "It's worth it. Don't you think?"

"I don't know if I can do it." And money—possessions—didn't mean that much to Eve. As long as she had food, clothing and shelter, she was content.

Carol shifted and gathered Eve's hands in hers and held them in her lap, an intimate gesture that unnerved Eve. "This isn't a job you pick. It's a job—a career—that picks you." The older woman reached up and touched a stray tendril of Eve's hair in a motherly way that made her heart ache. Eve feared she'd never connect to her own mother on this level. They lived in two separate worlds. "You're too good to give this up," Carol added.

Eve's stomach twisted. "I hate all the attention."

Carol leaned back and seemed to study her. "You have to dig deep. What got you involved in this career to begin with?"

Eve laughed, a mirthless sound. "I wanted to be a writer. Journalism seemed like a good major."

Carol waved her hand again, an overly familiar gesture. She leaned in and whispered conspiratorially, "You have too pretty of a face for that." Her mouth twitched. "You have been under a lot of pressure." She narrowed her gaze suspiciously. "You're not considering doing something rash, are you?"

Eve rubbed the back of her neck. "No, I..." Honestly, she couldn't voice what had brought her here today. Perhaps she felt adrift in Hunters Ridge, disconnected from the life she had built in Buffalo. But now that she was here, she couldn't be sure all the things she had worked for were what she wanted.

"Suze said your mother is ill. How is she?" Carol asked, changing the subject.

"I don't know. She needs lots of follow-up tests, but after the incident in the hospital parking garage she's too afraid to come back to Buffalo. I'm sure Suze told you about that."

"Yes, people have lost all sense of boundaries. I think it's because of the computer."

Carol automatically assumed the attack had been personal, because the man had recognized her from TV. Yet, Eve had no idea. Maybe it was random. The ever-present knot in her stomach tightened.

"You wouldn't have to go to the Buffalo hospital. They

have a satellite office in the Southtowns. Closer to…Hunters Ridge, is it?"

"Yes, but I like the doctor at Roswell."

"Oh, they have excellent doctors at the satellite and the doctors are always willing to consult."

Hope blossomed in Eve's belly. "That might work."

"I'll make a few phone calls."

Eve was about to refuse when she realized this might be the perfect solution for her mother.

Carol smiled, seemingly satisfied. "You asked me if all the attention in this job was worth it. This is what my career has gotten me. Not only money, but connections."

Eve nodded in agreement. Just then her phone started ringing. She ignored it, then it started ringing again.

Carol pointed at it. "Answer that, dear. Someone obviously is desperate to get ahold of you."

Eve felt her cheeks heat. Someone at Thomas's number had called three times. She swiped and held the phone to her ear.

"Eve! Eve!" Her stomach sank at the sound of Katy's frantic voice. "Is Mercy with you?"

"What? No, no."

"She's gone. We woke up this morning and she wasn't anywhere to be found. I thought she'd be home by now. Thomas didn't want me to call you. He didn't want me to give you the satisfaction. He thought you picked her up to get back at him for kicking you out."

"I would never do that." Eve stood, made an apologetic face toward her host, then stepped outside so she could talk in private. "Is Thomas checking with her friends?"

"*Neh*, he's convinced it's your fault."

The desperation in Katy's voice broke her heart. She thought of the turmoil she must have put her mother through when she ran away.

Her sister-in-law lowered her voice. "Can you drive around? See if you can find her. Maybe she's in town."

"I'm in Buffalo right now, but I can be back in about an hour."

"Thank you, Eve."

The fine hairs on the back of her neck prickled to life, as if someone was watching her. She dismissed the notion and slipped back into the house. She quickly texted Dylan to pick her up, then followed the sound of Carol's voice to her home office. She waited a beat until Carol ended the call, then Eve leaned on the doorframe. "Something came up. I have to leave."

"Oh dear, I hope it's not your mother."

Eve shook her head tightly. Carol reached for the phone. "I'll call you a ride."

Eve held up her hand. "One is on the way." She took a step back. "I'll let you make your calls. Thank you for taking the time to talk to me. I appreciate it."

"It was nice to see you." Carol's hand hovered over the phone. "You have a wonderful career in front of you. Don't let your nerves get in the way because that's all this is."

"I hope so."

"Keep me posted, dear."

Eve rushed to the front door, stepped outside and filled her lungs. She raced down to the circular driveway to wait for her ride even though she knew Dylan wouldn't be here immediately. The pool guy was loading his truck. When he stepped out from the back, they locked gazes. Eve's heart sank and a huge surge of adrenaline made goose bumps race across her flesh.

The man who attacked me.

Reflexively, she glanced down. Maybe he didn't notice her. She spun on her heels and ran up to the front door and twisted the handle. *Locked!* She heard fast footfalls on the pavement. She reached for the doorbell, but he was faster. He grabbed her ponytail. Her head jerked back as searing pain ripped the roots from her scalp.

"Leave me alone!" she screamed, panic making her nauseous.

Exploding pain tore through the back of her head. The ground rose up to crash into her face.

Darkness.

CHAPTER 25

When Eve didn't emerge from the stately home, Dylan reluctantly climbed out of his truck and went to the front door. The clacking of high heels followed the longest melody of a doorbell he had ever heard.

When the woman opened the door, she gave him the once-over before saying, "You're here for the...?" She seemed to be racking her brain, as if she should know why he was standing on her doorstep.

He smiled. Carol Oliver was definitely a woman who liked to be in control. In that moment, he understood why Eve sought her out for advice. "I'm Eve Reist's ride."

The woman's eyes flashed wide. "Eve? Oh, Evelyn." She tilted her head. "You are probably the most handsome hired driver." Her brow creased a fraction before smoothing. "Are you looking for a full-time job?"

Dylan held up his palms. "I'm afraid you've misunderstood. I'm a friend of Eve...Evelyn's. She let me know she was ready to go."

"Oh..." Confusion swept across the woman's face. "She stepped outside about ten minutes ago."

The first tingles of panic crawled up Dylan's spine. Eve had indicated she was worried about Mercy, but something else seemed off. He stepped backward and gestured to the side of the house. "I'll walk around the property. Maybe she's wandering around." He didn't wait for her to answer and he took off in a jog.

A few minutes later, he heard a door leading out to the back patio sliding open. Carol appeared in the doorway, her face under her mask of makeup having gone pale. "Um, you're going to want to see this." The anxiety rolling off her made his stomach knot.

Dylan followed the woman into a well-appointed mahogany office. She slid behind the desk and angled a large computer screen toward him. An image of the front porch was displayed on the monitor. Without being prompted, Carol pressed a few keys and Eve emerged from the house. Fourteen minutes ago. She was absorbed in her phone. Thirty seconds later, she appeared on the porch again. A split second after that, a man exploded onto the screen and yanked her back by her hair. He lifted something like a toolbox and brought it down on her head.

Panic made him light-headed and threatened to undermine his training. His cool composure.

Dylan stared at the screen as Eve dropped to the concrete. He moved closer and reached toward the screen with his fingers to trace her lifeless body, then pulled his hand back in a fist and slammed the desk. A few ceramic figurines that probably cost more than his yearly salary jumped. But to Carol's credit she remained silent, perhaps shocked by the display of events on her very own front porch.

"Do you recognize this person?" Icy steel laced his voice. The man hoisted Eve onto his shoulder and disappeared off-screen.

"He cleans my pool." Carol's voice cracked. She clicked a

few more keys and a pickup truck came into view on the driveway. The man had dumped Eve's lifeless body in the cab before jumping in the truck and racing down the long driveway. Carol yanked open a drawer and with trembling fingers sorted an array of business cards. She slapped one down and pointed at it. "This one. This is his card."

Dylan slid it off the desk. "Thank you." He pivoted and Carol must have read his hesitation.

"I'll show you out. This way." The woman moved quickly despite her choppy steps to the front foyer. "I'll call the police." She turned the lock and opened the door.

"Do that. Tell them everything you know. Meanwhile, I'm going to track Eve down." He slowed at the open front door. He pulled a business card out of his wallet and handed it to her. "Give this to the officer when they get here."

"I will." Carol seemed to compose herself, as if she had dealt with this type of situation all the time. "Go, go."

Dylan jumped into his truck and punched the address for the pool guy into the GPS.

He looked up and found Carol running toward him with an outstretched hand. He lowered the window. "It's her phone," the older woman said, her calm façade faltering. "It caught my eye in the bushes. Oh dear..."

Dylan grabbed the phone. "I'll find her." As he pressed the accelerator to the floor and he sped down the driveway, he sent up a prayer.

He couldn't lose Eve. Not again.

∼

A horrendous, nausea-inducing throbbing that made Eve want to gouge her eyeballs out of her head was the first horrible awareness as she emerged from complete blackness. The second was *Where am I?*

She slowly opened her eyes, bracing herself for the dagger-like pain that any light would be sure to induce. When it didn't come, she opened them a little wider. A soft light spilled out from not too far away, allowing her to take stock of her location, her situation.

She was in a truck, but she wasn't moving. In a garage, maybe. It smelled like stale takeout food and chlorine. She leaned forward and was pulled back by a seat belt. She rolled her eyes and immediately regretted it. Someone had knocked her over the head and had been thoughtful enough to buckle her in.

With a shaky hand, she reached for the buckle. That was when she heard arguing through the cracked passenger side window.

"You're such an idiot," an angry voice growled.

The hairs on the back of Eve's neck prickled to life with recognition.

"I didn't know. I freaked." Another voice, panicked, unfamiliar. "She saw me."

"You were not supposed to be seen. Ugh…"

Eve reached slowly for the door handle. She shifted and the subtle motion made her head explode in pain again. She couldn't process this. She couldn't process any of this.

She inhaled slowly through her nose to quell the nausea. She scanned her surroundings, careful not to move her eyes too quickly. Yes, she was definitely in a garage. She turned to look through the back window.

Ugh…her head.

The overhead garage door was closed. She still had to try to make an escape. She couldn't just sit here and wait for her attacker to return. The quiet click of the door amplified in the closed-in space, but the arguing continued unabated. She blocked out their angry words.

Gingerly, she slipped out of the truck and pushed the

door closed with a quiet click. The dome light seemed to take forever to go off. They didn't appear to notice. She crept between the narrow space behind the vehicle and the garage door.

Eve spied a person-door on the far side of the double garage and ran for it.

As she reached for the doorknob a voice called out. "Stop!"

Instinctively, Eve responded to the command and turned around slowly. Her stomach heaved with the sudden motion. Her closest friend was standing there with an angry scowl. Her eyes radiated an anger Eve had never seen. Something darker.

"You messed up everything!" Suze screamed, her face growing red. "Everything!" She charged toward Eve who held up her hands to block her.

~

Dylan was gunning it toward Chip Jennings' house—aka the pool guy—when he got a call. He didn't recognize the number. He clicked accept on the controls on his steering wheel. "Kimble."

"It's Carol Oliver." Her perfect diction allowed him to imagine her sitting behind a long, curved desk reading the news.

Dylan squinted at the amber light about to turn red and he muttered, "Come on, come on..." He was not going to get stuck at the intersection.

"I'm getting to the point. This is important." The woman's voice was tinged with indignation. Undoubtedly she thought his chant at the red light was directed toward her. "I checked all my cameras and I found my pool guy's vehicle pulling into the garage at my daughter's townhouse." Her voice cracked.

"I don't know what to think. I tried calling Suze's cell phone but she's not picking up."

"Did you call the police?" When she didn't immediately answer, he added, "Give me your daughter's address."

Carol rattled off her daughter's home address then cleared her throat. "I can't imagine what my daughter has to do with this, and I don't want to get her in trouble. You can handle this quietly, right?"

"This man brutally assaulted Eve—Evelyn." He bit back his answer.

"On your business card it says you are a sheriff's deputy."

"Call the police and do not call your daughter again." He fought to contain his anger. He needed the element of surprise.

Dylan ended the call and quickly punched the address into his GPS and let out a quick breath when he realized he was only five minutes away.

"Come on, come on," he chanted to himself. "Come on!"

∼

Suze stormed toward Eve, dragging her hand repeatedly through her hair. The sunlight streaming in through the garage windows reflected the indecision in her former college roommate's eyes.

Eve swallowed hard and tried to calm her rioting nerves. Everything was going to be okay. She held up her palms. "What's going on? What are you doing?"

A watery smile flashed across her friend's face, and she swiped at something on her cheek. "I took you in when you had nobody. I was your only friend. Without me, you'd have nothing. You'd *be* nothing."

Each comment was like a jab to her gut. *Is that how Suze*

views our friendship? Eve sniffed. "You're like a sister to me." She had to will the panic out of her tone.

Suze's eyes grew narrow. "Then why did you have to swoop in and steal my mother's affection? Take everything that was supposed to be mine?"

"I...I..." She couldn't wrap her head around a coherent thought.

"I...I..." Suze twisted her face in a mocking gesture.

Eve had seen her friend direct her pettiness toward other people, but never toward her. Suze had often tried to get Eve to join in, but instead she'd dip her head and turn away, ignoring this ugly side. The character flaw had seemed like a small thing in comparison to the friendship that had saved her from a very lonely period in her life.

Behind Suze, her attacker paced back and forth. Back and forth. His jerky movements and head snaps amped up Eve's nervousness. Could she open the door? Get away?

Suze cursed and shook her head, as if realizing she didn't have a way out of this mess.

"I don't know what's going on, but I won't tell anyone. No one has to know. Please, let me go."

Suze took a step closer and cocked her head. "No one has to know what?" Her question came out as a taunt.

Eve realized there was no correct answer. She squared her shoulders and said, "Leave me alone." She spun around and grabbed for the doorknob. The door was locked.

Her heart sank.

Of course it was locked.

Suze blinked and a slow smile spread across her face, the likes of which was more threatening than her ugliest scowl. She grabbed Eve's ponytail and yanked her head back. Instinctively Eve palmed her head, as if that would stop Suze from ripping out her hair.

Suze gave it a good tug then pushed Eve down. She

landed on the concrete behind the truck. "You surprised me, Eve. I thought you'd quit much sooner."

Eve slowly moved backward, scooting across the floor in a pseudo crab crawl. The meaning of Suze's words still not sinking in.

"I could see you writing off the creepy note left on your windshield or your flat tire, but when you stayed the course after the attack in the parking garage, I knew I'd have to step up my game."

Eve's mouth went dry as some of the pieces started to drop into place. "I thought we were friends." She had no idea Suze resented Eve's relationship with her mother.

Suze narrowed her gaze. "I thought when your mom got sick that maybe you'd run back to Hunters Ridge for good, but I had to make sure. That's why I sent Chip to attack you after the doctor's appointment I made. He was supposed to slice that pretty face of yours."

Eve's stomach ached as she slowly pushed to her feet. She planted a hand on the garage door to steady herself.

"*You said* you never wanted to be on camera," Suze snarled. "*You said* you didn't like the attention. *You said* you were *my* friend."

Eve swallowed around a lump in her throat. "All of those things are true."

"Then why did you take the job on *AM Morning*? I wanted to be the on-air talent. No one wants to be stuck behind the camera."

"I...you..." Eve blinked slowly, realizing she'd never get through to Suze, not when she was spiraling out of control. "You said you didn't care about that job. That you were only in the business because your mother forced you into it. I had no idea."

"Of course you'd have no idea about the pressure I was under. You're a stupid Amish girl."

Eve felt her face flood with color.

"My mother would toss you aside if she knew how ignorant you were. How unsophisticated. How simple."

Eve couldn't imagine Carol Oliver throwing those insults at her daughter. The older woman had been so kind to Eve. Or maybe she had been kind because Eve had accepted all her advice. Perhaps there was a side to the woman that Eve had never seen.

"I can fix this," Chip said behind her. He suddenly rushed to his truck and emerged with a knife, perhaps something he had used in his job. "If she's gone, we don't have to worry about her."

Suze's eyes grew wide and she turned. "Don't be an idiot."

Chip lunged and Suze seemed to make an instant decision and stepped between Eve and the man. The knife plunged into Suze's side. Her eyes widened and she grabbed her belly. Cherry-red blood oozed out between her fingers as Eve steadied her and they both sank to the garage floor.

"It's going to be okay. It's going to be okay," Eve repeated while she sensed a commotion nearby.

Chip had slammed the button to open the large door. It rumbled in its tracks on its ascent.

"Call an ambulance! Call an ambulance!" She choked out the words on a wave of fear and grief.

Chip jumped into his truck, and Eve dragged herself and Suze out of its path.

He jammed the vehicle into reverse and peeled out of the garage.

"I thought you were my friend." Suze stared up at her with unseeing eyes. Her voice had a faraway quality. Eve cradled her misguided friend's head in her lap. "*Carol* had to take you as her pet project. I wasn't good enough."

Eve glanced around desperately. Her friend needed help.

Just then an elderly lady walking her dog approached. "Call an ambulance. Please."

The excited dog yipped and yipped, scraping across Eve's already frayed nerves.

"They're already here." The little old lady waved her free hand above her head, apparently motioning someone over.

A truck skidded to a stop outside the garage followed by a couple patrol cars. Eve finally allowed herself to take a breath.

Dylan! It's Dylan.

He seemed to assess the situation. His eyes locked with hers and she had to fight not to sob with relief. "Are you hurt?" he asked, fear radiating from his warm brown eyes.

"No, no, but Suze…" Eve turned over her hands, red with Suze's blood. She was so overwhelmed with emotion that she felt numb.

Dylan tipped his head and gestured to the police officer. "Get an ambulance here. We have a…"

"She was stabbed." Eve glanced at the long, serrated knife on the garage floor.

"Knife wound." Dylan placed his hand on Suze's shoulder, but met Eve's gaze briefly before focusing on Suze again.

Suze sniffed. "I messed up."

"It's okay," Eve said, hoping, praying she was right.

"So, this is Dylan." Suze let out a laugh-cry. She looked up at Eve. "You are one lucky jerk."

Tears of nostalgia and pain prickled Eve's nose at her friend's jab. "Shhhh…everything is going to be okay."

CHAPTER 26

Dylan placed his hand on the small of Eve's back. "Come on." She stood frozen, her bloody hands out in front of her. "Right over here." He directed her toward a second ambulance. The first one had already left with Suze inside, lights and sirens blaring. "You're going to the hospital, too."

Eve glanced up at him, confusion and shock clouding her eyes. "I'm fine."

"You took a blow to the head. You need to get checked out."

"How did you know?"

"Carol Oliver has video cameras both at her home and her daughter's home. Otherwise I still might be going out of my mind searching for you."

Eve closed her eyes and lifted her hand, as if to rub her face, but then stopped and scrunched up her nose. "I need to wash the blood off." Her lips quivered and silent tears slipped down her cheeks.

"Okay," he tried to reassure her. "We'll take care of that.

You'll also have to give a statement to the police. But first, let's get you to the hospital."

Eve glanced at the ambulance, then leaned into Dylan. "Will you take me?"

"Of course."

He directed Eve toward a utility sink in the garage where she washed her hands. When he finally got her tucked into the passenger seat of his truck, she seemed to relax her shoulders a bit, some of the strain of the day draining out of her. "I can't believe Suze was behind this."

Dylan navigated around the police vehicles. "Suze and her mother's pool guy."

"She knew him. She sent him after me in the parking garage at the hospital."

"I thought you and her family were close."

Eve sniffed. "She was jealous of all the attention her mother gave me. Of my job promotion. I don't think she really wanted to hurt me. She wanted to scare me away from taking the job." She dipped her head and ran her hand through her hair, then pulled it away and studied it, as if worried it was still contaminated with her friend's blood. "Is she going to die? Oh, we have to notify her mother."

Dylan reached across the console and placed his hand on Eve's knee. "The police are taking care of that. You need to relax."

She laughed, a rueful sound. "I don't think that's happening anytime soon." She jolted up. "Oh my goodness—" She glanced around, as if she was looking for something. "My phone. My phone—I have to make a few phone calls. The contacts are in there."

"It can wait."

"No, you don't understand. Just before—" She closed her eyes and shook her head. "I got a call from my sister-in-law Katy. Mercy is missing."

"That's why you were worried about Mercy?" Dylan leaned over and tapped the glove box on his dash and the door popped open. Her phone sat on top of his registration and insurance papers. "Mrs. Oliver found it."

Eve grabbed it and met his gaze. "Thank goodness." Then her expression grew more somber. "I don't know what I'd do without you."

His heart tightened. He was praying she'd never have to find out, but they had a lot to wade through before they got to that point.

"How far are we from the hospital?"

"GPS says five minutes."

"I better hurry and make this call." She groaned. "Oh, my head is pounding." She glanced over at him and half her pretty mouth quirked into a lopsided grin. "When this is all over, I'm going to need a vacation from my vacation."

~

Eve swallowed down a new wave of nausea and focused intently on tapping in Annie Yutzy's name. She called the woman who had helped her leave the Amish seven years ago, and surprisingly found herself saying a silent prayer that she'd have some answers.

"Hello?" Annie's voice cracked. She sounded older than Eve had remembered.

"Annie?"

"Yes?" the older woman replied cautiously.

A wave of memories crashed down on Eve, but now was not the time for a trip down memory lane. "This is Eve Reist."

"Eve, dear, how wonderful to hear from you."

"I was hoping you'd have information for me."

Silence stretched across the line. Eve knew how protective Annie was of the young women she took into her care.

"I'm worried about my niece, Mercy Reist. Have you seen her?"

Another beat of silence.

"I promise I won't tell anyone where she is. I do need to reassure my brother that she's safe. You can trust me." Eve had a hunch that Mercy had found Annie's name in the journal.

"I don't know how she found me," Annie said quietly. "I haven't been taking girls in for a while now. My George has been sick."

"I'm sorry to hear about George." Eve had enjoyed watching the interaction between Annie and her husband. He had a wonderful sense of humor and seemed to love to make his bride laugh. They'd prepare dinner together and chat and laugh. They had a way of making their home feel so welcoming.

"We trust in God." The woman had left the Amish but had kept her faith. Eve was beginning to realize she should follow her example. Then, after a slight pause, Annie said, "Mercy is safe. Give her a night and then I think you should come and talk to her."

A weight lifted from Eve's chest. "Thank you, thank you, thank you."

"You're very welcome, dear. I look forward to seeing you and hearing what you've been up to."

Eve ended the call and shifted toward Dylan as the blue sign for the hospital came into view. She quickly dialed her brother's phone number but the voicemail was full. "I hope this doesn't take long because I need to go home and tell my brother that Mercy is safe."

To his credit, Dylan didn't ask a ton of questions and instead offered a solution. "I'll call Deputy Flagler. She can be at your brother's place in minutes. Let him know Mercy's safe."

As much as her brother was suspicious of law enforcement, she knew she had to let Katy know as soon as possible that Mercy was fine. "Thank you."

Dylan parked in one of the emergency room parking spots and jogged around to her side of the truck. He opened the door and helped her out. Conflicting emotions expanded inside her. They locked gazes and time seemed to slow.

Dylan tucked a strand of hair behind her ear and he smiled. "Don't scare me like that again."

"I won't." Eve leaned in and wrapped her arms around his waist and rested her head on his chest. "I promise."

His clean scent reached her nose and his solid arms held her tightly. She never wanted this moment—this feeling—to end. And for the next few moments, she shoved everything—Suze, Mercy, her job, her family—out of her head and took comfort in the arms of a man who always made her feel like she was right where she belonged.

He planted a kiss on her forehead. "You ready to go in?"

She shook her head and held him tighter. "Give me a few more minutes," she whispered, her face buried in his chest. "A few more minutes."

EPILOGUE

Four months later

Dylan stood in the small vestibule off the foyer of the church he had been going to since he was a young boy. He and Jacob used to play hide-and-seek while their mother cleaned the church. He slowed in front of the mirror, wondering how different things would have been if his brother hadn't broken his back. Hadn't gotten addicted.

He checked his tie for the tenth time and whispered, "I wish you were here, buddy."

A quiet knocking sounded on the door. "Come in."

Tessa peeked in. A curious line ran vertically between her eyebrows. "Is someone in here with you?"

Dylan smiled. "Just me."

Tessa stepped fully into the room. She had on a beautiful red dress and her hair was swept up. "You look beautiful." She ran a hand down the silky fabric. "Your fiancée has good taste. I always love a Christmas wedding."

Running feet sounded on the marble vestibule and grew closer. His nephews. Dylan's heart nearly exploded and he tousled Mason's hair and picked a piece of lint from the shoulder of Benjamin's black suit. "You guys look sharp. We're going to make a handsome trio up there."

"Mom said I get to carry the rings!" Mason boasted with his usual enthusiasm. The same enthusiasm in which he gave his new friends from preschool a tour of his orange and blue bedroom walls.

Benji frowned for the briefest of moments. "I'm not sure why he gets to. I'm the oldest. *He'll* probably lose them."

"No one's going to lose anything." Tessa patted her small purse. "I'm holding them until go time."

"Speaking of which…" Dylan tugged on the sleeve of his suit and checked the time. "Is Eve ready?"

Tessa smiled. "I was just downstairs with her. Yes, she's ready."

"Have my parents arrived yet?"

"Grandma thinks it's too cold out," Mason said. "She said we can go visit her in Florida and go to the beach."

"My parents raised us in Hunters Ridge and now it's too cold for them." Dylan followed Tessa's gaze to the small window. Big flakes of snow floated in the air.

"It's snowing!" Benji said. "Can we go outside and play after church?"

"One thing at a time." Tessa rolled her eyes and smiled.

Mason scrambled to get a closer look out the window and bumped the dresser. A tall vase with fresh flowers wobbled, then steadied.

"Come on, let's give your uncle some space," Tessa said. "This place is too tiny for you boys."

Dylan moved to the back of the church where he greeted a few last-minute arrivals. He'd glanced at his watch, wondering if he should enter the nave, when Deputy Caitlin Flagler breezed through the double doors.

"Brrr!" She shuddered as she slid off her winter coat and draped it over her arm.

At first, she didn't seem to see him standing off to the side. He stepped forward and waved. She jerked her head back. "You sure clean up nice," he said.

Caitlin touched her hair, hanging loose around her shoulders. She always wore it in a tight bun for work. "Why, thank you." She took a step closer. "And take a look at you. Eve must be something special to have gotten you to the altar so quickly."

Dylan shook his head. "I'm blessed she came back into my life."

"One lucky girl…" Caitlin let the words hang out there. Just then her phone began ringing in her coat pocket. She scrambled to find it and glanced at the screen. "It's the boss."

Dylan's heart spiked like it always did when it came to work.

"Sheriff?" Caitlin lowered her voice and stepped away from the church entrance. After a moment she came back. "Sorry about that."

Dylan tipped his chin in her direction. "What's going on?"

"It can wait." Caitlin smiled. "You're getting married."

"Don't leave a guy hanging."

"Okay." Caitlin's face lit up. "Early this morning Elmer Graber crashed his buggy. I arrested him for drunk driving." She lifted her hands. "There was this whole big scene." She lowered her voice. "I still think he was the one who left the slaughtered pig on Eve's porch. That kid's trouble."

"Eve doesn't want to pursue it. Neither does her family. You know that." Dylan wasn't going to let his frustration ruin his wedding day. "She doesn't want to cause any more stress for her family. That's probably the hardest part about being a deputy in an Amish community. They don't always want our help."

Caitlin playfully pointed at him. "This guy's up to no good. I'll get him on something."

"It's my wedding day. Let your hair down." They both laughed.

Caitlin patted his chest. "Congratulations, my friend. We'll have to solve crime another day."

"After my honeymoon."

A smile slanted Caitlin's mouth. "After your honeymoon," she repeated and hoisted the heavy coat draped over her arm. "Hopefully you're going someplace warm."

Dylan bit back a snappy reply, then nodded in silent greeting to Annie and George Yutzy as they made their way through the vestibule and into the main part of the church. "Go on in. It's almost show time."

Dylan walked up the aisle as the guests chatted.

He found Mason and Benji sitting in the front row with their mother. "How are my best men doing?"

Tessa smiled at her young boys with tears in her eyes. No doubt she was thinking of her husband, Dylan's brother, who would have been his best man.

"Okay, boys. Ready?" he asked, cheerily, trying to shake the weight of his loss.

Tessa slid the rings into Mason's suit coat pocket. Then she brushed a kiss across Dylan's cheek. "I'm so happy for you." Then she met his gaze. "Be happy."

"I will." He swallowed around a lump in his throat. "Thank you."

The processional music started and Dylan took his place in the front of the church with his nephews. The doors swung open and a wave of affection Dylan had never known washed over him at the sight of his beautiful bride. Years ago when he met the sweet Amish girl in the movie theater, he could have never imagined this.

When Eve reached him, he took her hand in his and gently squeezed it. His heart was ready to explode. "Thank you for making me the happiest man alive."

"What a wonderful day," Eve said to one of her guests at the reception, probably for the hundredth time, but she couldn't help herself. She was happy and content to her very core.

She hooked her arm through Dylan's and pulled herself closer and stole another kiss.

She scanned the reception room to see everyone—well, almost everyone—she and Dylan knew, gathered to celebrate their special day. She slid her hand down to his and threaded their fingers. "Let's go visit with my mom for a bit."

Dylan dutifully followed her across the room to where her mother and Mercy, dressed in their Sunday dresses, sat at a table with a beautiful flower centerpiece. The pair represented her entire family. Eve slid into a seat next to her and Dylan gently squeezed Eve's shoulder, then kissed his mother-in-law's cheek. "I'll be right back."

Eve watched her husband join a few of the deputies by the bar. Then she turned her attention back to her mom. "You must be tired." They had learned her mother had breast cancer, and thankfully, she had agreed to undergo treatment. The doctor had given her a hopeful prognosis, and Eve was feeling gratitude for one more blessing in her life.

"A little tired, but I'm fine." No doubt, the arthritis they had discovered—and that had been causing her mother so much pain—was also wearing on her.

Mercy leaned over from her seat on the other side of her grandmother. "Our ride will be here shortly."

Eve lifted her gaze to her niece. "I'm so glad you both were able to come."

"I'm sorry my *dat* and *mem* didn't come."

A soft sadness pinged Eve's heart. "Baby steps, right?" Her brother, at least, hadn't tried to forbid their mother and Mercy from attending the wedding.

"We don't need to discuss that now," her mother said. "Eve and Dylan will be here in town now. Perhaps time will soften Thomas's heart."

Eve smiled. "I'll still take you to your appointments. Marriage doesn't change anything."

"Marriage changes a lot of things."

"Not that."

Her mother tapped her knee. "And I get to see my daughter raise her children here in Hunters Ridge."

Eve suspected things wouldn't be as simple as that, but it was a hopeful beginning. "Dylan and I will be back from our honeymoon with the new year. Thankfully, you don't have another appointment until after the holidays."

Mem waved her hand. "Let's leave that business for another day."

"I love you, *Mem*."

"I love you, too." Her mother cupped Eve's cheek. "I'm glad you found a *gut* man. Now go be with your handsome husband."

Eve stood and had started to walk away when Mercy caught up with her and surprised her with a heartfelt hug. "I'm so happy for you. Maybe someday I'll find someone like Dylan."

Eve jerked her head back. "I thought...wait, what?"

Mercy had run away to Annie Yutzy's home after learning in Eve's journal about the elderly woman's work helping young Amish women transition to the outside world. As it turned out, Mercy didn't actually want to leave the Amish, she only wanted to make an impression on her father. She had been so frustrated that Thomas had so willingly pushed his sister away that Mercy had hoped he would have a change of heart when he realized his stubbornness might cost him his oldest daughter, too.

When Mercy returned from two nights away with the

Yutzys, their family had a long discussion about Mercy's future. Thomas finally decided he wouldn't pressure her to marry Roy Brenneman, allowing her to find another suitable Amish man. With everything else going on, Thomas realized that was a battle he wasn't willing to fight. He'd rather see his daughter baptized in the Amish faith than lose her entirely. Perhaps her niece's bold move had softened her brother's feelings toward Eve. A fraction, at least, as evidenced by Grandma Gerty's and his daughter's presence at her wedding.

Mercy laughed. "A new Amish family moved into the old Mullet family home. Their oldest son came to the Sunday singing a few times." Her face blushed a pretty pink. "He drove me home last week." She pulled up her shoulders and let out a quiet squeal.

"You deserve good things," Eve said.

"Maybe you can meet him."

"I'd like that."

Mercy looked like she was about to say something else when Carol Oliver caught Eve's eye across the room. Eve hadn't planned on inviting her friend's mother to the wedding, but she had practically invited herself when she learned about the impending nuptials. Carol had called Eve to try to convince her to reconsider her career options. Perhaps she had regretted her decision to back Eve and not her own daughter in the career department.

The older woman seemed to be taking everything in. Her nose scrunched up, perhaps an indication that she didn't approve of Eve's church basement reception.

When Carol found Eve looking in her direction, her expression suddenly smoothed. She lifted her hand and waved breezily. "Beautiful wedding, dear. But I'm afraid I must be going. I have a long drive home."

"Thank you for coming." She smiled tightly and hesitated

a fraction, then asked, "How is Suze doing?"

"Better." Carol shrugged and Eve let it drop. Suze had survived the knife attack in her garage and had been admitted to a psychiatric center instead of jail. Her accomplice Chip was in jail awaiting sentencing. "The girl never was cut out for this business."

Eve found herself bristling at the woman's cold assessment of her daughter. Eve wanted to tell her that Suze had only wanted her mother's approval. That Suze's attempts at scaring Eve into quitting—since she already knew how much Eve disliked being in the public eye—were as misguided as Carol's attempts to force Eve into the spotlight by using her connections in the business.

"I wish her well," Eve said instead.

Carol blinked a moment, and for a fraction of a second Eve saw her facade fall. Then, just like that, it was back in place. "Evelyn, dear, if you ever get tired of this small town, I can make a few phone calls. Get you back on TV." She tilted her head knowingly. "You're really good, you know that, right?" She waved her hand around. "We could even control the narrative. Top anchor grew up Amish." A perfectly groomed brow drew down. "It would be a fascinating feature."

"I thought you said we should never be the story."

"Oh, but this would be different."

Eve's gaze drifted beyond Carol to Dylan who was smiling at her. Her heart warmed. "I think I'll be perfectly happy here. My first love has always been writing." Maybe she'd finally have time to do that blog justice. She still had that post she wrote that first night back in Hunters Ridge sitting in the draft folder. "I have an idea for a novel."

"Mmm..." Carol's serious gaze turned warm. "I hope you find everything you were looking for here. Congratulations, dear."

Carol turned to leave and Eve threaded her way through the dwindling crowd to her husband. She sagged into his arms. "Can we leave before the last guests leave? Would that be rude?" she whispered into his neck and he pulled her closer.

"Hmmm…" He tipped his head toward the exit. "I don't think anyone would blame us."

Heat crept up her cheeks and she laughed. "If you asked me last Christmas what I would be doing this Christmastime, I would not have guessed this."

"What do you think we'll be doing next year at this time?" Dylan asked, meeting her gaze.

Eve looked up, taking in the twinkling lights and imagining her future—their future. Would they be starting a family? Would they have built the home of their dreams they'd been talking about? Would her brother be more welcoming by then? Then she laughed softly and brushed a kiss across his cheek. "Let's enjoy the moment."

Dylan gently tucked a strand of hair behind her ear, leaving a trail of shivers in its wake. "I am. Absolutely." His deep voice rumbled over her. "Now, let's get out of here."

NOTE FROM ALISON STONE: I hope you enjoyed the 4th book in the Hunters Ridge series. I'm excited to announce that **Plain Survival**, the next book in the series, is coming Winter 2021.

Please consider signing up for my newsletter if you want to hear about upcoming books, new releases, and deals on my website: AlisonStone.com. Thanks so much!

Meanwhile, turn the page if you'd like a sneak peek at **Critical Diagnosis**, a stand-alone romantic suspense.

SNEAK PEEK: CRITICAL DIAGNOSIS
CHAPTER ONE

"Three Saturdays in a row." James rested his hip against the desk in the cramped nurses' station and met Lily's gaze. His close-cropped hair made him look every bit the Army captain he was. "I appreciate it. The patients appreciate it. It seems more and more people are counting on this clinic." He tossed the medical chart on top of the pile, a satisfied smile on his handsome face. A day well spent. The chart teetered. Lily lunged to grab it. James did the same, his solid hand brushing against hers, but he was faster.

"Oh, boy—" Lily McAllister dipped her head and tucked a strand of hair behind her ear. "I don't want to be around if those charts hit the floor and all the files scatter." She stood and divided the pile in two, stacking them neatly next to one another. Stepping back, she planted her fists squarely on her hips. "There."

James laughed, his white smile bright against his tanned skin. "Nancy would have my head on Monday. She already gives me a tongue lashing when I file the charts. Apparently, I'm messing with her system. I guess it takes more than a month for the new guy to figure out *the system*. Even though I was the one who set up the system before I enlisted in the Army. Go figure."

Lily lifted her palms in an I-totally-had-nothing-to-do-with-it-if-the-files-get-messed-up gesture. "I'm just the weekend help." She scooted out from the confined space and leaned her elbows on the counter. "It feels fantastic to escape the research lab and actually practice medicine. It's been a long time."

"I appreciate the help." He lifted his eyebrows and bestowed his best persuasive smile. She had seen it before. "You on for next Saturday, too?" The free health-care clinic was obviously short on staff. While the man running it was obviously short on tact.

Mirroring his raised eyebrows, Lily slid off her stethoscope and slipped it into her bag. "I'm beginning to think you're taking advantage of my good nature."

A mischievous glint lit his eyes. "Never. Think of the fine people of Orchard Gardens who count on this clinic." He leaned in closer. "Who count on you."

"Captain James O'Reilly, is this how it works in the Army? You say jump and people ask how high?" She rested her chin on the heel of her hand.

"I'm not in the Army now, am I?" He winked. "How about it? Next Saturday? Call it a date?"

Collapsing her arms on the counter, she dropped her forehead onto her arm. Lifting her gaze, she found him watching her. "Well," she said with an air of being put upon, "since you asked so nicely." A flicker of a smile teased the corners of her lips. She'd fail miserably as an actress. Good thing she had succeeded beyond her wildest hopes as a researcher. Regen, her research, was currently in clinical trials. She could finally breathe. She was this close to getting a treatment on the market for the disease that had killed her mother and afflicted her niece. It had been the culmination of years of hard work and the answer to a zillion prayers muttered into her wet, tear-stained pillow. So it only felt right to give back to the small community where she had been afforded so much.

Lily tapped the counter with the palm of her hand. "I'll make sure all the medicine cabinets in back are locked. You got the front doors?" They both had to be at James's grandfather's eightieth birthday party in a couple hours.

"Sure." The single word came out clipped, as if he were biting back further comment.

Lily strode down the long corridor of Orchard Gardens Clinic. Once a stately Victorian, it had been converted into a medical practice by James's parents, both physicians, when James was still learning how to color between the lines on the pages of his Bible-themed coloring book.

James had returned home to carry on the tradition after serving as a physician in the U.S. Army for the past several years. She wondered how long he'd have time for the clinic considering the rampant rumors floating around town. Apparently, James was slotted to head Medlink, the pharmaceutical company his grandfather had founded. Many speculated the elder O'Reilly's health was deteriorating.

The small town was short on physicians, but not on rumors.

She pushed open the last door on the right. The high-pitched creak and the chill from the air pumping out of the AC unit perched in the window made her skin prickle. Hurrying her pace, she secured the drug cabinets, turned off the printer and the AC. Her ears buzzed with deafening silence.

A banana peel in the garbage caught her eye. Unsure the janitor was scheduled over the weekend, she decided to tug out the liner and toss it into the Dumpster. If she didn't,

SNEAK PEEK: CRITICAL DIAGNOSIS

come Monday morning, a ripe banana would be a nasty surprise.

Voices reached her from the front of the clinic. A last-minute patient must have come in. She angled her head and noticed Mrs. Benson who had been in earlier with her two-year-old granddaughter Chloe due to an ear infection. Perhaps the sweet child hadn't settled down quickly enough for the elderly woman. Not wanting to disturb them, Lily headed toward the solid-steel door retrofitted for the building's second life.

The clock marked the hour with a soft chime. Six o'clock. Butterflies flitted in her stomach. Dr. Declan O'Reilly was due to arrive at the party at eight. That meant she had to arrive before then or risk ruining the surprise—and Mrs. O'Reilly's wrath. She hustled down the short flight of stairs. She twisted the thumb-turn, releasing the dead bolt. The back door opened onto a small parking lot. For the briefest of moments, she tilted her face and basked in the warm summer sun.

She'd be locked out if she let the door slam. A broom rested against the back wall, a perfect wedge. She set it in place and then headed toward the Dumpster in the far corner of the lot.

A tall row of evergreens separated the clinic's property from a squat row of brick apartment buildings. A car sped past on the country road out front, the boom-boom-boom from its car speakers vibrating through her.

Clamping her mouth shut, she grabbed the small, black door on the Dumpster with the tips of her fingers and pulled. The door slid in fits and starts, getting hung up in its tracks. *Ugh.* Flies and an acrid smell hovered over the steaming pile of trash. Her lungs screamed for fresh air. She tossed the bag inside. It landed with a squishy thud.

The deep hum of an engine idling near the apartments

SNEAK PEEK: CRITICAL DIAGNOSIS

seeped into her consciousness. Backing away from the rancid Dumpster, she drew in a breath and peered through the branches. A beat-up, lime-green car with one of those do-it-yourself paint jobs was parked on the other side. Her pulse whoosh-whooshed in her ears, as if God whispered a warning.

Get back inside where it's safe.

Yet she dismissed her paranoia. The small town of Orchard Gardens was one of the safest towns in America to live. It said so on the quaint sign on the main road into town.

Yet instinct urged her on. She spun on her heel and hustled toward the back door of the clinic. The trees rustled and solid steps sounded on the hard earth behind her. Her gaze darted toward the tree line. Heat swept up her neck, her cheeks. A man, his baseball cap slung low on his forehead, strode toward her. The menacing expression on his hardened features annihilated any doubts. He was coming toward her.

Her vision narrowed.

Move faster.

Get inside.

Slam the door.

Want to read more? Kindle and paperback of Critical Diagnosis are available now on Amazon.

ALSO BY ALISON STONE

The Thrill of Sweet Suspense Series

(Stand-alone novels that can be read in any order)

Random Acts

Too Close to Home

Critical Diagnosis

Hunters Ridge: Amish Romantic Suspense

Plain Obsession: Book 1

Plain Missing: Book 2

Plain Escape: Book 3

Plain Revenge: Book 4

Plain Survival: Book 5

A Jayne Murphy Dance Academy Cozy Mystery

Pointe & Shoot

For a complete list of books visit

Alison Stone's Amazon Author Page

ABOUT THE AUTHOR

Alison Stone discovered her love of writing romantic suspense and cozy mysteries after leaving a corporate engineering job to raise her four children.

Constantly battling the siren call of social media, Alison blocks the internet and hides her smartphone in order to write fast-paced books filled with suspense and romance

Married with four (almost) grown children, Alison lives in Western New York, where the summers are gorgeous and the winters are perfect for curling up with a book—or writing one.

∽

Be the first to learn about new books, giveaways and deals in Alison's newsletter. Sign up at AlisonStone.com.
Connect with Alison Stone online:
www.AlisonStone.com
Alison@AlisonStone.com

CPSIA information can be obtained
at www.ICGtesting.com
Printed in the USA
LVHW082136300523
748472LV00028B/747